A
CHRISTMAS
REVELATION

For a complete list of Anne Perry's Victorian mysteries, including the Monk series and the Pitt series, as well as her many other novels, visit:

www.headline.co.uk
www.anneperry.co.uk

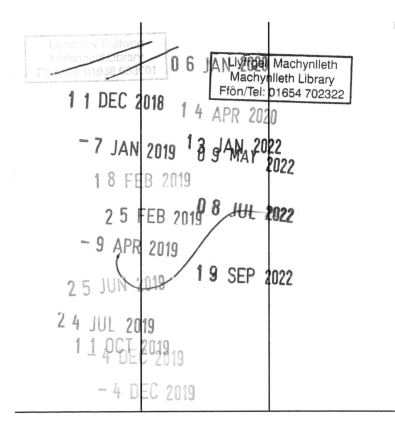
Dychweler erbyn y dyddiad olaf uchod
Please return by the last date shown

LLYFRGELLOEDD POWYS LIBRARIES

www.powys.gov.uk/llyfrgell
www.powys.gov.uk/library

4721800048985 9

Anne PERRY

A CHRISTMAS REVELATION

HEADLINE

First published in 2018 by
HEADLINE PUBLISHING GROUP

1

Cataloguing in Publication Data is available from the British Library

ISBN 978 1 4722 5736 9

Typeset in Times New Roman PS by Palimpsest Book Production
Limited, Falkirk, Stirlingshire

Printed and bound in Great Britain by CPI Group (UK) Ltd,
Croydon CR0 4YY

Headline's policy is to use papers that are natural, renewable and
recyclable products and made from wood grown in well-managed
forests and other controlled sources. The logging and manufacturing
processes are expected to conform to the environmental regulations
of the country of origin.

HEADLINE PUBLISHING GROUP
An Hachette UK Company
Carmelite House
50 Victoria Embankment
London EC4Y 0DZ

www.headline.co.uk
www.hachette.co.uk

To all those who wish to belong

Worm stood and stared, overcome with wonder. She was the most beautiful woman he had ever seen in all his nine years of life. She was like sudden sunshine on a dark day – all light and warmth, softness, the place you looked because you couldn't help it. She walked the way everybody should: gently, head up, smiling. Maybe other people looked like her at first glance, but when you looked again you saw she smiled, not as if there were something funny, but as if she knew something good that she could share, if you would stop and listen.

But no one did. They all walked past her about their business, hurrying on as though they were late, or afraid they might miss something. There were carts of vegetables for market, a large brewer's dray with magnificent horses, brasses gleaming, a barrow boy selling apples, and a hansom cab, the driver flicking his long whip above his horse's ears, as if it could go any faster in that traffic.

The lady was speaking to a man with one leg. He was leaning on a crutch, awkwardly, and trying to fish in his pocket with the other hand.

The lady smiled and said something. She picked a second bunch of white heather from the tray suspended around the man's neck, and put her other hand gently on his arm, to stop him looking any further for change.

He could be a soldier from the Crimean War. Worm knew about that. Of course, it was twelve years ago now – 1854–56, long before Worm was even born – but those who saw it and those who didn't see it – they had still lost someone, and they didn't forget.

The lady with the light in her face was moving away now. The one-legged man smiled as he watched her go and, without thinking about it, Worm followed her. He had no idea where she was going, but he wanted to look at her a little longer. He wouldn't get lost. He had always been somewhere around here, close to the river, until early last summer when someone had found him and taken him to live in the clinic in Portpool Lane. He had fended pretty well for himself on this bank, picking up bits of coal, or even brass when he was lucky, and selling it. He knew his way around.

Claudine would be cross with him for being late, but after telling him off a bit, she would forgive him. She always did. Even when he hadn't had a front tooth, the smile always worked. His new teeth were almost grown through now.

The lady was moving quite quickly. He nearly lost her. He might have done, except that the clouds parted for a moment and a shaft of sunlight fell on her, making her hair bright for an instant. Worm pushed past a man in a heavy topcoat, just in time to see another man with grey hair walk up to the lady and put a hand on her arm.

She flinched, as if he had gripped her too hard, and swung round to face him, anger in her eyes. Then, as though steeling herself, she stood a little straighter, and said something to him that Worm was too far away to hear, but it was clear from her face that she was angry.

The man's expression became a twisted sneer and he pulled her towards him. No one else in the crowd took any notice. Was it a private quarrel with her father? Or an employer? Her clothes were ordinary, it was only her grace in wearing them that made them look good.

The man pulled her again, roughly. She resisted, and with her free hand slapped him hard across the face. Then instantly she looked terrified, as if realising what she had done, when it was too late.

He was furious. He snarled something.

Worm ran forward, shouting, 'Stop it! Stop it!' loudly. Maybe there was nothing he could do, but he could try. He could kick really hard! And if he got hold of someone's hand, he could bite. He charged at the man, head bent down to butt him in the stomach.

At that moment, another man appeared, quite a lot younger. He was taller and slimmer, and clean-shaven.

'Fool!' he shouted at the older man, and before the older man could confront the lady again, or Worm could kick him in the stomach, the younger man had pulled the lady out of the way. She fell forward against him, and he put his hand on her and twisted her round, pulling her with him. She struggled for only an instant, then seemed to give up the fight and follow obediently. Perhaps she was afraid of being hurt again, or worse?

The older man swore, then followed after them. Nobody appeared to have noticed Worm. He squeezed

4

between two women with bags of laundry. They were so deep in conversation that they only swatted at him with one hand, for his impertinence, without missing a word.

He could still see the older man and he ran after him across an open space in the street, just behind a costermonger's barrow full of vegetables, and in front of a hansom whose driver was shouting at everyone to get out of the way. Might as well yell at the incoming tide, Worm thought, but some people felt better for complaining. Gave them the idea they were doing something.

He could still see the older man as he turned a corner into an alley. Worm usually had more sense than to go into dark corners, but this time there was no help for it. He ran past an old woman with a dog, swerved round the corner, and thanked whatever heaven there was that the older man was still in sight, and not far ahead. He had caught up with the younger one, who was still holding on to the lady. Was she all right? Had they hurt her again?

If he didn't want to be seen, Worm should hang back. But if he did that, he would not know which way they had gone. What use was following anyone if he did not go all the way? He walked quickly. He was quite quiet because his boots were very thin anyway, one stage before getting actual holes. He did not like to tell anyone at clinic because he knew they needed all the money for the sick people. It was a pretty big thing that they gave him food every single day, and a bedroom of his own, with a real bed in it, and blankets. He knew enough not to be greedy.

At the end of the alley, they turned left. That was inland, away from the river. Worm did not know this area so well. The river was his; at least it used to be. Now he lived inland a bit, and west of the patch of the bank he knew best. This was going east and inland, towards Mile End.

Still, he had to find out where they were taking the lady. He followed them silently for what seemed like a long time. He could still see her. He couldn't see if she was struggling, or if they held her so tightly that she couldn't struggle. She must be frightened.

He was catching up. He moved quickly, darting in front of a wagon and causing the driver to yell at him a string of imaginative abuse. The older man turned round, maybe at the colour of the words. For a moment, his eyes met Worm's. Worm froze. The wagon passed so close to him that the driver reached out and cuffed his ear. It stung, but Worm ignored him.

The older man, still holding hard on the lady's arm, shouted at Worm, 'Get out of 'ere, or I'll tan yer 'ide till it falls off yer skinny bones!'

The lady turned and she saw Worm. There was recognition in her face. She remembered him. She opened her mouth as if to say something, but the younger man pulled her so hard she staggered against him.

A group of people with a vegetable cart passed in front of Worm, and when he looked again, the pavement was empty. The lady was gone, and so were the two men who had taken her.

Worm spent a long time looking for them, but he found no sign. Did that mean they were inside a house near here? He couldn't ask anyone: 'Have you seen a lady who smiles, with the sun in her hair? And two men who were taking her somewhere she didn't want to go?'

There was nothing to do but go all the way back to the clinic, where at least he would get something to eat. He was hungry and cold, and his legs ached. There was definitely a hole in his boot now, and it was going to freeze tonight. But what could you expect? It was nearly Christmas.

He turned round slowly and started to walk westward. He would strike a main street he knew before too long.

*

Squeaky Robinson was in his office, working on the account ledgers for the clinic in Portpool Lane, when Worm returned. Squeaky was in his sixties; he declined to be more exact than that. He was always exact with money, however, to the farthing. But with age, anybody's age, such precision was not necessary. He was quite tall, but scrawny, and he wore a black frock coat, year round, whatever the weather. He had a lugubrious face, teeth that did not even appear to possess any order at all, and white hair that straggled on to his shoulders. His bookkeeping was skilled, inventive and meticulous.

In the past, he had owned these two large houses in Portpool Lane and run them as a thriving brothel. But he had been tricked out of ownership by the lawyer Sir Oliver Rathbone, and permitted to stay in residence, since he had nowhere else to go, only on condition he kept the accounts for the new owner, and ran the place as a clinic for street women – prostitutes of greater or lesser degree – who needed medical help. This was all the plan of a woman who used to be an army nurse in the Crimea with Florence Nightingale. Mad as a hatter, she was, but brave. Squeaky would give her that. Actually, he would have given her just about anything she asked for, but, thank heaven, she did not know that.

Squeaky had protested the injustice of the whole arrangement for several years, on and off. Now it was off. Too many people realised that he actually enjoyed it. It was too much to say he was respectable. It would sound like an obituary! But he had moments approaching respectability.

He looked up as Worm knocked on the door and, without waiting for an answer, opened it and came in. He looked tired and bewildered, and he almost tripped over the loose part of the sole of his boot.

'What is it?' Squeaky asked. It was hard enough to have the place turned into a virtual hospital; he would not have it turned into an orphanage as well!

Worm closed the door and stood in front of it. He looked small and very miserable. It occurred to Squeaky that he was doing it on purpose. He had survived alone on the Thames bank for a long time; making people sorry for him was probably how he had achieved it.

Worm drew a deep breath. 'I saw a lady taken away by two men. She didn't want to go, but they made her. I was too far away to help, but I followed her to see where they took her. I know where it is … sort of … nearly …'

What on earth should Squeaky say? He looked at Worm's face and knew there was no point in arguing with him. It was significant that he hadn't gone to Claudine Burroughs with this mystery. It was she who had insisted that Worm stay here. But that was women for you! Sentimental. 'Specially about children. She spoiled Worm. Always giving him food …

Claudine was a highly respectable, middle-aged woman – actually more than respectable – she was well-to-do, almost rich. Heaven knew why she wanted to spend her time in a place like this, when she had a rich husband and a fine house somewhere! Actually, Squeaky knew why, but he pretended not to. It was … kinder. No one wanted to admit to loneliness. He had despised Claudine when he'd first met her. He had told the Crimean nurse that Claudine was worthless.

But then a strange thing had happened. He had discovered that Claudine was far more valuable than he had assumed, and more generous in her judgements of others – and of Squeaky in particular! Any woman of character would loathe her mean-spirited and domineering husband. She was better off here, and she knew it.

But Claudine would not be any help in this situation, and probably Worm knew that. That was why he had come to Squeaky.

Squeaky should have been pleased. He wasn't. Worm was only being practical. It was not that he had any deep trust in Squeaky.

Worm was waiting, the bright hope slowly fading from his eyes.

'Sort of?' Squeaky said, his wild eyebrows raised.

'Yeah. I followed them to the street where they disappeared.'

'Disappeared?' Squeaky said sceptically.

Worm swallowed. 'Went inside somewhere.'

'What street was that?'

'I don't know. But I know where it is! I can take you there ...'

'Oh? And what would I do when I get there? Assuming that you could find it again?'

'I *could* find it!'

'For what?'

'To find her! Rescue her from those men. They're going to ...'

11

'What?' Squeaky was making excuses. He knew it and, what mattered, Worm knew it too. Squeaky was honest to a fault. Except when he was deliberately dishonest, and that was always for a reason. 'Worm, there isn't a thing you can do about it. Maybe they're her brothers? Or one of them is her husband?'

Worm had no family to compare the idea of relationships with. His face filled with confusion, and a kind of disappointment that the idea seemed to be so ugly.

Squeaky was immediately sorry. 'Most families are good.' The words stuck in his throat. He had no family either. Never had had, so far as he could remember. He chose not to try very hard. 'But there are bad people.' This was ridiculous. Worm knew that, for heaven's sake. 'People lose their tempers!' he added sharply. ''Specially if they're scared. Maybe they thought they'd lost her!'

'She weren't lost,' Worm insisted.

'How do you know?'

A sweet smile of memory lit Worm's face. ''Cos she was smiling. Just standing there, all bright in the sun. And happy.'

'There's no sun today. It's December!' Squeaky replied. And then the moment the words were out of

12

his mouth, he regretted them. He had spoiled something unnecessarily. 'Not here, anyway.' He tried to
fish it back. 'Maybe where you were.' He refrained
from asking where Worm had been, and why.

'She weren't lost,' Worm repeated. 'And she didn't
want to go with them. They pulled. Hard! They held
on to her, so she had to.'

Squeaky tried to find a way out of this before it
was too late. 'You don't know what happened,' he
pointed out. 'We can't all go around the streets
knocking on doors, and asking if anybody's quarrelling. They probably all are, one time and another.
And it ain't none of our business.' He had a sudden
idea. 'And if they think she's been telling other people
all about family troubles, they'll really be angry with
her. Telling tales on family is real bad.'

Worm stared at him.

'If Miss Claudine were to make a mistake, or break
something precious – if there was anything precious
here – would you go and tell people?'

'No!' Worm was indignant. 'Course not!'

'See?'

'Oh.'

It was time to change the subject, before Worm
could think about it too hard. 'Sometimes you get

lost and you don't want to be found, but sometimes you do. It's what you get lost for,' he added. Actually, his mind was going back to the time Claudine had made a foolish mistake, had left the clinic and became lost. It was Squeaky who had found her. He could remember the incident well. She was miles from the clinic, cold, wet and scared stiff, all huddled up like a child. When she'd recognised Squeaky, to her embarrassment she had wept with sheer relief. He still felt a strange pleasing warmth inside himself when he recalled her face. It was the first time either of them had seen the other as a person, with feelings they could understand. She was not a sarcastic wealthy woman, who had condescended to help the poor, to prove to herself and her neighbours that she was a Christian, whatever that meant. She was a lonely woman imprisoned in a purposeless marriage, without joy, without even honest affection.

And he was not a worthless, scruffy ex-brothel-keeper who was not to be trusted in anything, least of all money. Ever since the day Oliver Rathbone – beg his pardon, *Sir* Oliver Rathbone – had entrusted him with the bookkeeping, Squeaky had accounted – and honestly – for every penny.

'Christmas is coming,' Squeaky said, changing the

subject to rid himself of the sense of being out of control of his own life, and the feelings that caught him unaware. 'We've got to do things.'

Worm blinked and looked puzzled. 'Why?'

'Because Christmas is special! It's different from all the rest of the year.' Squeaky spoke as if that were self-evident, but actually he was struggling to think of a good reason, other than that people needed a cause to celebrate. It was dark most of the day; in fact it was the darkest, bleakest time of the year. The cold was biting. Sometimes there was snow, but that; pretty as it was, brought its own troubles. When it melted it was grey and sludgy, and unbelievably wet. It was a very good time to have a festival. And Christmas was a terrific festival. There were decorations, music, church bells ringing, good things to eat, and people were nice to each other for three days or so, especially to strangers.

Worm was still waiting. He knew nothing of Christmas and was about to ask about the lady with the bright hair again.

'You give presents to people.' Squeaky, reading Worm's thoughts, continued with the first thing that came into his mind, determined to distract the child. 'Things you think they will like.'

15

Worm's eyes widened. This sounded promising. However: 'What about the lady?' he asked. 'What if it wasn't her husband or her brothers what took her away?'

'You listening? Christmas is more important'n anything. You wrap the presents up,' Squeaky continued, 'in coloured paper and ribbon, so they look nice.'

'Who do you give them to?' Worm asked. 'Does it have to be family?'

'Course it doesn't!' Squeaky dismissed the idea with scorn. Having never had a family himself, he was aware with a peculiar hurt that Worm hadn't either. A child should have a mother, at least! 'Some of the best ones are to friends. Or even to people you just like.' He made it up, stretching for ideas. 'Or to someone you don't know very well, but would like to make them happy. You don't even have to put your name on it.' He saw Worm's horror. 'Usually you write who it's for, and who it's from, but you can do it without saying who you are, just "A friend".'

Worm smiled slowly. Squeaky thought he knew what Worm was thinking, but some thoughts should be allowed to be private.

Squeaky hurried on. 'And you decorate the place: the rooms and sometimes a bit outside, like a wreath on the door.'

'What's a wreath?' Worm asked.

'It's a circle woven of leaves and branches. About this big.' Squeaky held his hands up, about two feet apart. 'And you put ribbons on it, red ones, red satin ones, and sometimes holly, with berries, red berries, sometimes tinsel, that's strips of silver stuff. It shines in the light.'

'And you put it on the door? Outside?'

'Yes.'

'I never saw one. Who'd have money to spare decorating a door?'

'Well, you will this year! That's what we've got to do. You and I.' That should take his mind off the woman in the street! And it would be good for the patients, if there were still any here at Christmas. Decorate the place. Why not? There was little else for lonely people to do in the grey days of mid-winter. They should make a big thing of it. Make a Christmas pudding. And a cake! Tie red ribbons around the place. He even knew somewhere where they sold red candles. To hell with the budget. If rich people could enjoy Christmas, they could make themselves feel righteous by giving a little extra to the clinic funds, come the New Year.

'And red candles,' he added. 'And Christmas pudding.'

'What's that?'

'Like spotted dick.' He mentioned the rich, light sponge pudding full of raisins he knew Worm was familiar with. 'Only ten times as good.'

Worm looked at him with quite open disbelief. Nothing could be ten times as good as spotted dick.

'You'll see,' Squeaky said, hoping to heaven he could pull it off. Broken promises to a child were terrible. Close to beyond forgiving, especially if they were about Christmas.

'Are we going to do that?' Worm asked. His voice was full of doubt.

'Didn't I just say so?' Squeaky demanded.

Worm took a deep breath, nearly spoke, then changed his mind.

That was it. The decider. 'Well, don't just stand there!' Squeaky accused. 'We must start. First, we must get the decorations. We need tinsel, lots of it, and we need ribbon and coloured paper to wrap things up in. And red candles. White ones are ordinary, good for every day, but not for Christmas. And pine cones.'

'What do we need pine cones for? What's a pine cone?'

'Don't interrupt. It's a thing that grows on a pine

18

tree. I suppose we need a pine tree, too.' He glared at Worm for bringing up the subject. Now he was going to have to get a tree! And that was all Prince Albert's fault, bringing German ideas into England, just because he had married the Queen! Poor man was dead anyway. Sending people cards was probably a German idea, too.

'Do you eat them?' Worm interrupted his train of thought again.

'Eat what?'

'Pine cones.'

'No, you decorate them, and they smell nice. Don't just stand there. We have a lot to do. We need to make a list.' Squeaky considered ordering Worm to write it. He could write, after a fashion – that was Claudine's doing, too – but it wasn't always legible. Perhaps this wasn't the time to push him. 'I'll do it,' he added. 'You help me think of things. Go and fetch the chair and sit down.'

Worm did as he was told and sat obediently, watching Squeaky all the time. This was a side to him Worm had never seen before.

Squeaky wondered what on earth he was doing. But it was too late to turn back now. Please to heaven Claudine would accept the idea, and allow him to use all the money. And their donors would somehow replace it for the necessary things, like food, and medicine, and firewood.

'Why do we decorate things with ribbons?' Worm asked.

The wretched child had an endless curiosity and seemed to imagine Squeaky knew the answer to everything.

'Because they're pretty,' he said tartly, writing 'RIBBONS' down on the page, and then, on the next line, 'TINSEL'.

'Why red?' Worm asked.

'Because it's pretty!' Squeaky snapped. 'It's a happy colour!' His glare defied Worm to argue.

Worm nodded. 'Why are we happy at Christmas? Is it just to make ourselves feel better, when everything's freezing and there are no flowers and things?'

'No! Of course not. It's …' Squeaky had to struggle to give an answer that made sense to a child who had never had a home he could remember, or anyone who loved him in particular, and certainly no religious teaching. All his life's experience would make the traditional stories seem ridiculous – and painful. Actually, that was pretty well what Squeaky had found. But looking at the hope in Worm's eyes, he couldn't say so. What was he expecting? Miracles!

'A long time ago, hundreds and hundreds of years, even thousands,' he began, and it sounded hollow already. He started again. 'A very long time ago, a special baby was born. He was supposed to save the world, and people, at least some people, knew that he was going to. All sorts of different things happened that had never happened before. There were lights in the sky, angels, some people said. And music. Angels sing, did you know that?'

Worm shook his head.

'Well, they do. And shepherds, who lived outside to look after their sheep, saw this and heard what they were singing ... or anyway, they understood it. They knew this baby was born. Actually, he was born in a stable. You know what a stable is?'

'Course I do. It's where horses live. They have them behind big houses, so they can keep their carriages for when they're going out.'

Clearly the idea of being born in a stable did not seem odd to Worm, in fact he could well have been born in one himself. It would have been better than a crowded and filthy slum.

'They went to see the baby,' Squeaky went on

quickly, scraping his memory for details of the Christmas story. 'And there were three Wise Men also, came from some place far away. They rode camels.'

'What's a camel?' Worm asked.

'It's a big animal you ride on. They don't have them in England, and don't interrupt! The Wise Men brought presents to the baby. That's why we give presents to people now. They brought very precious things because they were rich, but it doesn't matter what you bring, as long as you think the person will like it.'

'Was there a horse in the stable?'

'Of course!' Squeaky had no idea, but it seemed like a good thing. 'And the camels, too. It was a big stable. All sorts of creatures knew that this baby was special, even though most people didn't.'

'How?'

'How what?

'How did they know?'

'Because animals understand what God is saying a lot better than people do!' How in hell do I know? he thought. Worm seemed perfectly satisfied with that. Squeaky moved quickly to more modern celebrations, where he was on safer ground. 'You've

22

heard the bells at Christmas? Church bells, not just like any Sunday?'

'I think so,' Worm agreed.

'And you've seen the carol singers, and heard them?'

'Yes.' This time he was certain.

'Were they singing songs about the baby, and Christmas, the Wise Men and all that?'

'"I Saw Three Ships" …' Worm said.

'What? What have three ships got to do with it?'

'They sing about three ships coming in,' Worm said patiently. 'What does that mean?'

'I've no idea. We'll find out. If anyone knows. Are you finished interrupting me?'

'Yes.' Worm's eyes never moved their steady gaze. He hardly even breathed.

Squeaky began to feel self-conscious. He became aware of just how little he knew about Christmas. It wasn't just folklore, tradition, what people said and did because their parents had, because it made them feel good. 'All these things have meaning,' he asserted. 'But mostly we've forgotten what it is. It reminds us that he came for all of us without exception, so we should try to be more or less nice to everyone.'

Worm looked sceptical.

'I said try!' Squeaky told him stiffly. 'And we are going to start with Miss Claudine, and then spread it out to everyone who is here at Christmas time. You hear me?'

Worm smiled. 'Yes, what are we going to do?'

Squeaky had absolutely no idea. 'We are going to have a special dinner. We are going to decorate with candles and ribbons … and … things. We are going to make certain no one is left out. No one at all. And we are going to sing carols and … I don't know what. I haven't decided yet.' Then he had a sudden idea. 'Perhaps we'll make a Nativity scene!'

'What?' Worm was totally confused, but he looked happily expectant. He trusted Squeaky, and that was very unnerving.

Squeaky struggled to remember exactly what went into a Nativity scene. There had been one in the church he could remember in his childhood. He could still see the mother and child quite clearly in his mind's eye. And the donkey, and the two or three lambs. Were the people shepherds, or kings? Kings would be more fun! 'There will be in it the people who come to see the new baby, who know how important he really is,' he replied without hesitation.

'Why is he important?' Worm asked immediately.

'Because he's going to do ... something ... so we could all be forgiven for what we do wrong, if we are sorry.' That sounded incomplete, but as close as Squeaky could get. He had a generally sour view of religion. In his opinion, it made people self-righteous, lacking in humour or kindness, and very prone to sit in critical judgement of just about everyone else. Of course, there were exceptions, but they didn't usually bring religion into it. They were just nice, and the religion was incidental. It was part of who they were.

Worm was staring at him, not yet satisfied.

'He was so ... gentle ... he could understand everybody.' Squeaky reached frantically into his mind for an explanation he could believe. How could he expect Worm to believe it, if he didn't himself?

'How could he do that?' Worm asked.

Squeaky was not sure if Worm was curious, or if that was doubt in his eyes. 'I told you, he was very special. When you get to like people, you listen patiently and try to understand. And when you really understand, you don't always agree, but you like them anyway.'

Worm nodded slowly. Apparently, he accepted that. 'What happened to him?' he asked.

Squeaky swore silently to himself with several words he did not want Worm to hear, although having grown up on the dockside, he probably already had. Maybe he did not yet know what they meant. 'That's a whole 'nother story,' he said. 'I'll tell you that at Easter.' That was neat!

'What's Easter?'

'Next year. Now be quiet! Christmas first. Now I've lost my place.'

'We are going to make a … some kind of a scene, whatever that is,' Worm reminded him instantly.

This time, Squeaky thought before he spoke. 'It's of the stable, and the baby, and the people who came to visit him.'

'How did they know?'

'I already said! Because there was an especially bright star in the sky. You could see it from anywhere.'

'Anywhere in the world?'

'Yes.'

'Oh. The world is round, like a ball, did you know that?'

Of course he knew that. But he had not known that Worm did. 'Yes. And it turns round and round, all the time,' he said. He was not about to be tested on astronomy by a nine-year-old! 'But the Three …'

Had he said Kings or Wise Men? '… Kings did not come from the other side of the world. They rode on camels.' At least they had in the pictures Squeaky could vaguely remember.

'How do we get camels?' Worm asked.

'We don't! They left the camels outside!' Squeaky snapped. 'We will have to ask the women to help us make the people. And the animals. That can be their job. We have to have everybody help, or it won't be their Christmas, too.'

'Who else is there?'

'The baby, and his mother, and father. Some shepherds. And the Three Kings.'

'That's good. Do the Kings wear special clothes?'

'Of course. Everybody dresses up in their best for Christmas, whatever that is. If it's your best, then it's good enough.' He was going to settle that before it got any further. 'But the ones that matter most are the baby and his mother.'

'Is she beautiful?'

Before Squeaky could answer, Worm continued, 'I know what she looks like. She's smiles and … and there's light in her hair.' He blinked as if his eyes were full of tears but he was determined not to show them.

So he had not forgotten the woman in the street. Damn! Squeaky would have to think of other Christmas stories to tell to take Worm's mind off that damn woman! A ray of winter sunlight seemed to have ignited some dream in the child! 'Among other things …' he scrambled to think of them. What stories had he heard as a child, or any other time, for that matter? The Three Kings had brought presents. What were they? '… gifts,' he said. 'Wonderful gifts, with special meanings for his life.' Now he had to think of them. He seemed always to be digging himself further in.

Worm sat on the edge of his chair, listening as Squeaky recited the adventures of the Three Kings. Sometimes he called them Wise Men, but he meant the same people. Sometimes he referred to them as Magi, but Squeaky didn't know what that meant. Worm knew that, because when Squeaky didn't know something but was making out he did, he had a habit of fidgeting with his left hand, curling and uncurling his fingers. He was making it up about the places the Three Kings visited on the way. But he was quite sure about the star, and about the gifts being important. He insisted there were things that told about the special boy's life, and what it was going to be.

Gold, because he was a king, too, but not of any country specially, but everywhere and nowhere. Frankincense, which had something to do with priests, and myrrh, which was something to do with death. It was all very strange, and didn't make a lot of sense, but Worm could tell that Squeaky believed it, so he didn't want to upset him by asking. And Worm was quite sure Squeaky believed in the woman, the mother of the special baby, with the sun in her hair, like a golden light shining, too. He wanted it to be true, and he believed in so little that Worm wouldn't take that away from him. It would hurt, and Worm did not want to hurt him, so he listened to all the stories, no matter how unlikely they were, about kings and shepherds and angels and all sort of things.

Eventually Claudine came and interrupted them to say that it was suppertime.

'We're planning Christmas,' Squeaky told her.

Claudine was a tall woman, not pretty, but comfortable to be with. Worm liked her voice. It was soft, and even when she was annoyed, which wasn't very often, it still sounded nice. And she liked him. She always liked him, even when he was clumsy, or forgot things, or deliberately did something he was told not to. She would punish him, but she still liked him. It was about the most comfortable thing in the world that there was someone who always liked you.

Now she looked surprised. 'Planning what, exactly?' she asked.

'A goose,' Squeaky replied, without hesitation. 'Perhaps two. How many people are going to be here … about?'

'About ten,' she answered. 'Maybe twelve. And add a couple more if there are fights, or it's very cold and we get people frozen. You'll need two geese at least. I suppose you want me to cook them!' It was impossible from her expression to tell if she was going to agree or refuse. Or set some condition on it.

'Thank you, Mrs Burroughs,' Squeaky said graciously. 'I knew you would help us. I told Worm you would.' That was a lie. He had never said anything at all. Actually, he had not even mentioned the goose, or two.

Through supper, held in the kitchen, like all their meals, Worm, Squeaky, Claudine, Ruby – who had been a maid here so long she thought of it as home. Perhaps she didn't have any other? – and Miss Bellflower, the current cook, all spoke about Christmas and what they would do.

Claudine hesitated over the expense. Worm could

see the doubt in her face when Squeaky talked about decorating with ribbons and bells and candles, and tinsel and even a tree. His voice grew in enthusiasm as he went on. He began by playing to his audience, but halfway through he was playing to his own imagination. Or was it memory? Watching him, Worm could not tell, and it would not only be rude to ask – or as Claudine said, impolite – it would be cruel. People needed to pretend sometimes. Worm knew that. Down on the dock at night, he had hugged an imaginary blanket around himself, and heard the crackling of flames in an imaginary fire.

He watched the faces of everyone around the table, and wondered if goose was really better than hot cottage pie, or if people just thought it was because they wanted to. Cake was another thing. That had to be special.

But it was the red ribbons and the idea of a tree that made the girls' eyes shine. Once or twice he sneaked a sideways look at Claudine, and it was other people's excitement that pleased her. It was there every time someone else came up with a new idea, but there was also fear in her, from the way she looked at Squeaky, half in gratitude and half in anger, that he should take such risks, which gave away what

31

she was thinking. It would be cruel to let them all down.

*

Worm slept soundly that night, but he woke early in the morning thinking again of the lady he'd seen yesterday in the street with the sun in her hair. She had been frightened when she went with the two men. It was in her face, and the way she pulled back from them, even though her feet went forward.

He should have done something. He lay on his back in the dark, with the blanket pulled up to his chin, and thought about it. Finally he got up and found his clothes in the dark, put them on, then opened the door to let the light in from the passage. He could find his boots easily enough without any light. He had a lot of walking to do today. He shouldn't think about it or he might get scared and stay in the warm.

He put them on and tied them up, then crept out, closing the bedroom door behind him. Everybody would think he had slept late.

Downstairs in the kitchen, the big clock said five something. Nearly six. He had time to get a piece of bread from the larder and a little bit of meat dripping to go with it. It tasted salty and meaty and buttery, all at the same time.

He finished it and went towards the back door. His boots sounded as loud on the floor as a horse's hoofs, but that was just because he was alone and doing something Claudine might disapprove of. Actually, everybody would disapprove of it!

He had unlatched the back door and had his fingers on the handle to open it when he felt a hand on his shoulder. It scared him so badly, he shouted aloud. He had heard nothing, nothing at all! His voice sounded like a scream.

'And where do you think you are going?' Squeaky asked softly in his ear.

It took Worm several seconds to get his breath back, never mind his voice.

'Well?' Squeaky insisted. 'Back to bed – with your boots on?' Now there was sarcasm in his voice.

Worm's mind raced. What were the risks of a lie? How much did Squeaky know, anyway? The long fingers were gripping his shoulders harder. He settled on the truth. 'I've got to find the lady. I know where she went.'

'In the dark?' Squeaky asked sarcastically. 'You

didn't know if you could find it yesterday, even in the daylight.'

'It'll be daylight by the time I get there. It's ...' He looked at the clock. 'It's nearly six.'

Squeaky was silent for so long, Worm thought he might have got the time wrong. But he was sure the little hand was the hours, and the long one the minutes.

'Then I'll come with you,' Squeaky said at last. 'God only knows what you'll get into by yourself. Come on, then. You can't go through the door! You'll have to open it!'

Worm looked away from him, afraid he might change his mind. He opened the door. It was stiff, and in his impatience Squeaky yanked it from him and swung it wide. The outside air was freezing cold, and there was a rime of ice on the steps. It would be slippery.

They went out together, closing the door silently behind them, and set out down Portpool Lane, then turned to the east, and into the wind off the river.

'I suppose you know where you're going?' Squeaky asked.

'Yes.'

'And how you're going to get there?'

Worm hesitated. 'No …'

'Thought not. But I know. You were going to beg and finagle your way!'

Worm had no idea what finagling was, but clearly it was not good, from Squeaky's tone. There was not the time to argue, or say it was unfair to use words nobody understood. It could even be made up. 'How arc we going?' he asked, with as much innocence as he could manage. He was quite good at that.

Squeaky avoided an answer. 'Where did you first see her? We'll start there.'

'Surrey Docks,' Worm answered. 'I know right where.'

'And they went inland?'

'Yeah. Into Limehouse.'

'Then we'd better start at Surrey Docks. If we don't find her body, that's it. We've got other things to do. How am I going to get all the ribbons and bells and candles, not to mention the cake and the goose, if I'm traipsing around the alleys of Limehouse?'

'Miss Claudine is going to make the cake,' Worm pointed out, running a step or two to keep up.

'Out of what?' Squeaky said.

'I don't know!'

'Out of flour and eggs – lots of eggs – and butter,

and currants and raisins and sultanas, and spices, and all sorts of things. They don't grow in cupboards, you know!'

Worm ran another couple of steps. 'You don't have to come with me. I can find my own way.' It was hard to say that. He needed Squeaky – he knew that now – not only to get there but to help the lady if she was in trouble. He was not a bit frightened when he thought about it. Well, only a little. But he could feel his throat go tight.

'Keep up!' Squeaky said sharply. 'Stop talking, and save your breath to walk!'

Worm did not answer, but he kept silent as ordered, and actually Squeaky did slow up a bit. The sky was beginning to get a little paler in the east, as if they were always travelling towards the light. Worm was happy not to talk for a bit. It was nice not to be alone, and even if Squeaky was cross at coming with him, that was nothing unusual. Squeaky was always cross if he was taken away from his papers and his figures. He said he was interrupted, but he still took every opportunity to stop. Like it was something nice to eat and he didn't want it to be over.

He was very clever with figures. He could add up anything, or subtract, and quickly. In fact, he could do it in his head. He knew what the numbers ought to be, and he knew if they were wrong, the way some women could tell a lie just from your face.

Worm could not always tell a lie from the truth, but he pretty well could say if a person was happy or miserable, whatever they pretended. Like now – Squeaky was only pretending to be really annoyed. He was walking quickly and lightly, and humming a little tune to himself. He even snatched Worm's hand when they crossed a busy road, then let it go again instantly, as if he wished he hadn't. Worm didn't mind. He didn't want to get lost; he had no intention of slipping away. It was almost like they belonged. He was pleased now that Squeaky had found him in the kitchen.

It seemed as if the whole city was waking up. It was getting lighter all the time. They passed several groups of workmen calling out to each other. There were lots of carts of vegetables in the road.

They came out of Grey's Inn Road at High Holborn. That was a really big street, going east and west. Squeaky bought them a cup tea each from a woman with a stand. For once, he didn't argue the price. It was a bit too strong, and not terribly nice, but Worm enjoyed it. He stood on the icy pavement beside Squeaky and sipped from the cup. He could feel it trickle down his throat with its heat spreading out through him. He wasn't even hungry. Well, not very. He had missed Claudine's breakfast of hot porridge, and that was a pity, but this was a duty that could not be missed. The woman with the light in her hair might need their help, and there was Christmas to go back to.

After the tea, they caught an omnibus all the way to Cheapside, and then another one towards the Tower of London. Squeaky told him that was where they put traitors, even royal ones. That's where they had chopped off the head of Queen Elizabeth's mother, Anne Boleyn, among others.

Squeaky was full of stories. You could tell from his face whether he was enjoying it or not. The lines curved upwards. But that didn't necessarily mean the story was true. He enjoyed the invented ones just as much. Worm knew he would have to play along, but most of the time he didn't have to pretend: he loved stories.

It was well into Limehouse by the time they got off the last omnibus and stood on the narrow pavement and watched the horses pull away.

'That's heavy,' Worm remarked, looking at the bus.

'How can the horses pull that many people? Don't they get tired?'

'No. They're like you and questions,' Squeaky replied. 'Only time you stop talking is when your mouth is full, and not always then!'

Worm did not reply, but increased his pace as he recognised the corner of the street they were on. He looked both ways, let a wagonload of wood go past, then darted across to the furthest corner. He heard Squeaky shouting behind him and slowed up a little. This was one of the corners he had passed yesterday. But from which way had he come? Only then would he be certain, or almost certain, which way he had gone. He turned around slowly, and came face to face with Squeaky.

'I don't know!' he said, for a moment afraid they were going to give up.

'I can see that,' Squeaky replied. 'If you can't decide, we'll try one, and then the other.'

A wave of relief engulfed Worm. Squeaky wasn't going to try and make him give up. Worm wanted to thank him, but he was afraid to say anything at all and perhaps make Squeaky think again. He set off along the pavement to the right, looking at every shop there was. He might remember something in a window.

Except that he had been watching the lady, and the two men who walked on either side of her, holding her savagely.

He had to look down at where he was going. The pavement was pretty rough, narrow in places, and there were broken stones. Perhaps he would remember some of those? It was almost daylight now and shadows were exaggerating everything. Nothing seemed familiar.

'I think it was the other way,' he said at last, stopping outside a barbershop. It had a red and white pole, which was bent where somebody had hit it. He would remember seeing that before.

Squeaky went back without comment.

They walked for nearly half an hour before Worm finally knew they were at the right place. The woman and the two men had disappeared somewhere along this street, except it had looked cleaner yesterday. Worm stood on the pavement staring at the buildings all around him. They were grey, ordinary, their tired-looking roof slates crooked. They were all about three or four storeys high with narrow windows, some of them broken and boarded up. Here and there the guttering had come loose from the walls. It would be dripping, if it were not frozen. But a glance at the stained walls told him where the water had run down over the years.

It was too early in the day for many of the chimneys to be showing smoke, but it would come. There would be thick grey plumes of it from those lucky enough to afford fires.

Worm felt Squeaky's hand on his shoulder, surprisingly gentle.

'This the place?'

'Yeah.'

'Do you know which door?'

Worm waited a moment. 'No,' he admitted. He looked at Squeaky, afraid to ask but willing him to try them all.

It might be only this once, all future favours rolled into one, but he nodded. 'We'd better try them all,' he conceded. 'Come on! Don't stand there!' Squeaky turned and walked smartly to the first door, leaving Worm behind.

Squeaky knocked on the door twice really loudly. Several moments passed and he was about to knock again when the door opened and a tired-looking woman stood there. Her hair was tied up in a knot behind her head, but dozens of strands fell out. 'Yes?' she said wearily. 'We'll pay you when we can!'

41

An unreadable expression crossed Squeaky's face. Worm did not know whether it was annoyance, impatience or pity.

'Don't want money,' Squeaky replied. 'You owe us nothing. I'm looking for two men, an older one and a younger one, and a young woman who's going with them against her will. Down this street. You know everybody around here?'

'Pretty much, but I mind me own business,' the woman replied.

'It's important.'

'Yeah?' She did not sound interested. Maybe she had too many problems of her own to care about other people's. She looked as if she had not energy to spare, even if she wanted to.

Squeaky fished in his pocket and pulled out a shilling. It could have been a loaf of fresh bread, from the look on the woman's face. 'Who lives up and down here?' Squeaky asked again. 'Who lets rooms? Which houses might be empty?'

She gave him an immediate list, from memory, of every house and who lived in it, and of the empty ones, what was wrong with them: drains blocked, roofs leaking too badly, rats, too many windows broken. She took the shilling before he had time to

42

change his mind, thanked him, and shut the door sharply.

Squeaky stepped back with a smile. 'Maybe lies,' he warned, Worm now at his heels, 'but it's a place to start. Poor creature. Probably got no business to mind but other people's. We'll try this side first.'

'Why?'

'Because any woman'll be at the back of the house, in the kitchen. It's one room you keep warm, even if it's only to cook there now and then. Coal and coke out there, and rubbish. Backyard fence.'

'Backyard fence?' Worm asked. 'What use is that?'

'To lean over while you gossip with your neighbour, of course! What did you think?' Squeaky said tartly.

That had not occurred to Worm. He had never lived in a house. Everybody in the clinic was too busy to gossip. And if you wanted to, there was enough going on inside to please anyone. Maybe it would be lonely in a house?

He followed Squeaky from one house to another while they made enquiries. He was beginning to run out of hope when a door was not opened, even though they heard voices inside. Worm crept up to the window. He was just tall enough to see over the sill.

It was only the middle of the day, but one of the lights was on, casting a yellow glow around itself. He could see a man's head, dark hair untidy, beard hiding his mouth. Was it the younger man of the two who had taken the lady?

'What are you watching?' Squeaky demanded from behind him. 'Who is it?'

'It's him!' Worm replied. 'I think ...'

'Is it or isn't it?'

'Wait!' Worm watched as the man moved. There were paintings on the wall behind him, and the wall was a beautiful pale red. The light glittered, as if it were ringed around with crystals.

A second man came into the part of the room Worm could see. Now he was sure: it was definitely the older man. He could see the white in his hair, only in the light it looked silver. Where was the lady?

'It's them,' Worm said in a whisper, as if they might hear him, even through the glass.

They were shouting at each other, he could hear that, although not what they were saying, except a few odd words. Without the middle bits they didn't make sense. It all looked warm with the flicker of firelight just beyond what he could see. There were pictures on the walls: greens and blues, not just greys.

He couldn't see the floor to know if there were carpets, but there might be, in a room like that.

Where was she, the lady with the sun in her hair? There was no point if she was not there! Suddenly the warmth drained out of Worm and he was just a little boy clinging outside someone else's window, a long way from home.

Even Squeaky did not speak.

One of the men shouted very loudly, just one word, and it wasn't in English. It sounded like 'eez'.

A door opened at the far side of the room. Worm could see only half of it, but it was enough. The lady came in. She looked exactly the same as he remembered her, and the light from the lamp shone on her hair just the way the sunlight had.

Worm let out a sigh that fogged the cold window, so for a moment he couldn't see anything at all.

'It's her!' Worm said, so quietly he could hardly hear it himself. 'She's there.'

Squeaky stayed well out of the way of the window. 'Sure?'

'Yes!' He was sure. The two men looked roughly the same, but he was absolutely certain it was her. In the whole world, there could only be one like her.

Something was happening inside. The younger

45

man was shouting and it was so loud that Worm could hear the words, even through the glass.

'Tell us! Now!' He reached out, took the woman roughly by the arm and swung her round to face him.

Worm raged with anger but he could do nothing but watch. Squeaky was standing right behind him now, holding on to both his shoulders. If anyone in the room had turned to look at the window, they would have seen them.

But they didn't.

The woman shook herself free and said something angrily to the younger man. He reached out to her, but the older man shoved his hand away. He turned to the woman again and said something in a low voice. She bit her lip, and seemed to give in. They all went out of the room.

Squeaky pulled Worm away from the window.

'No!' Worm tried to get himself free.

'Quiet!' Squeaky hissed. 'Come away from there! Do you want them to know we're watching?'

'They can't see through the walls!' Worm said angrily. 'They've gone. Where've they gone to?'

'Maybe out of the other door,' Squeaky said. 'Now come round the corner. If they go somewhere, we want to be able to follow them.'

'Can't we rescue her?' Worm begged.

'Why should she think we're any better than they are?'

'Of course we—' He started to say, but he had to admit there was no reason. She had seen Worm only once, an urchin who had smiled at her.

Whatever else he was going to say was interrupted by the front door opening and all three of them coming out on to the footpath. They walked straight past Squeaky as if he were a pedlar selling something they did not want.

'We going?' Worm whispered urgently. 'We'll lose them otherwise.'

'In a minute,' Squeaky said quietly. 'Not too close, or they'll know. Just wait!'

Worm shifted his weight from one foot to the other, but he could not move until Squeaky let go of him. When he did at last, the two men and the lady were already round the corner.

At last Squeaky went forward, and by the time they turned the corner, the three ahead were only just in sight. Squeaky's hand still rested heavily on Worm, so he was reduced to an unwilling walk.

They followed the three of them ahead for so long it seemed as if they were never going to arrive anywhere. Worm was tired and cold, and hungry. But the longer they watched the three people, the more they saw of the relationship between them, and the more puzzled they became.

The two men clearly wanted the woman to tell them something. They were alternately pleading with her and then threatening her. They were almost back on the street where they had started when finally the older man actually struck her across the face. It was not very powerful – it did not knock her off balance – but it left a red mark on her cheek.

Worm started to cry out, but found himself muffled by Squeaky's hand over his mouth.

Worm considered biting him, but apart from the fact that he was held too hard, he really didn't dare. He thought of kicking, but he didn't dare to do that either.

The lady's face bore the mark of the blow. She swayed a little, then slowly she smiled. Worm could hear her words, even from a distance. 'I'll tell you when I'm ready. When I'm sure.' Then she snatched her hand away from the older man and turned to walk along the street, going away from him with a very slight swing to her step.

The two men looked at each other. The older took a step forward, but the younger one grabbed his arm and held on to it. He swung round until they were facing each other. 'Wait!' he said fiercely, almost threateningly.

They stayed frozen, face to face. Then slowly the tension eased out of both of them and they went forward, following the woman along the pavement and then back to the house they had come from. They passed her as they reached it.

Squeaky and Worm were just in time to see them turn in at the doorway, fish for a moment for keys, and then let themselves in. They left the lady behind outside and she stood there in the street.

Worm made as if to run towards her.

'Wait!' Squeaky held him by the collar.

'What for?'

'Watch. You don't want to upset them for nothing,' Squeaky said sharply.

'I don't care …'

'They're closer to her than we are!' Squeaky hissed. 'Watch.'

The lady stood on the pavement only a moment longer, then pushed the door open and went inside. It appeared to close behind her, but made no sound.

Worm turned to Squeaky, frowning. 'Why did she go in? She could have run away!'

49

'How far would she have got?'

'She didn't try!' Worm protested.

'We don't know anything about her,' Squeaky pointed out.

'She was frightened, I know that.' There was absolute certainty in the set of Worm's jaw, and in the blazing clarity of his eyes. He was so young – and so sure.

Squeaky sighed. He had come this far. If he dragged Worm back home, he would only come back here the moment he was let go. Only this time he would be alone, and who knew what kind of trouble he would fall into? The best that could happen would be getting cuffed around his ear and told to mind his own business. The worst he didn't even want to think of. Who would miss one river urchin more or less? The thought made him feel ill. 'Well, she isn't frightened now,' he said. 'She gone in there and she didn't have to, so she must have a reason. One that we don't know about.'

Worm looked at him, his eyes clouded.

'So we get to find out then, don't we?' Squeaky said in exasperation.

Worm breathed in and out. 'Yes. How do we do that?'

Squeaky had no idea. 'We go and have lunch, and

we think about it. We listen. Maybe people know
who they are.' He was trying to think as he spoke.
If they were villains of some sort – petty thieves,
forgers of papers or of money, pamphlets, confidence
tricksters of some sort – he knew enough people
from his past to be able to find out. If they were
respectable, he would be very surprised indeed. What
troubled him was the fear that the woman was also
no better than that. Then what could he do to protect
Worm from having his dreams crumble in front of
him? Why did he have to be so innocent? He should
have known better! Damn it! He was nine years old.
Had experience taught him nothing?

'Do you really want to know?' he asked more
sharply than he had meant to.

But Worm did not hesitate. 'Course I do. We got
to ... to save her! She's frightened of them!'

'Maybe. But it doesn't seem they've hurt her yet.
She just went inside when she could've run away.'

'D'yer think so?' Worm asked.

Squeaky bit his tongue. 'Are you coming for something to eat or not?'

'Yes.'

'Good. Come on, then. We passed a pedlar with
hot pies a quarter of a mile back.'

'What if she comes out?'

'If she comes out and offers us hot pies, we'll take them!' Squeaky snapped, and, grabbing Worm by the shoulder, he half dragged him along the pavement.

Worm ate three pies, and would have eaten a fourth if Squeaky had been willing to buy another, but Squeaky was afraid he'd be sick. When they were finished, Squeaky went to the nearest public house and started asking questions. Then he went to the pawnshop, where he had an acquaintance: a very disreputable one that he would rather Worm did not know about, and would definitely rather Claudine didn't.

He was cross with himself. What did it matter what this nine-year-old urchin thought of him? He could see a good woman in distress in what was actually a couple of rough pimps picking up one of their tarts who had got above herself. She might well be afraid of them if she'd taken the whole of her earnings, instead of giving them their cut. And of course she would go back with them. It might be an abusive relationship, one sided, but she could not do without it. He did not want to explain all this to Worm. Let him keep his dreams a little longer.

This was not the time Squeaky wanted to explain to Worm how he knew so much about the business of prostitutes, and the men who looked after them and lived on the proceeds of their trade. Those days were long behind him. It had not been his choice to leave them; it had been Oliver Rathbone's decision. But Squeaky had made the best of it, and he was just about respectable now. He would never tell Rathbone, but he was secretly grateful.

So he told Worm to wait outside the pawnbroker's, and on pain of not being helped any more, to be there when Squeaky came out. He went in and the man he expected to find was behind the counter. He paled when he recognised Squeaky.

'What do you want? I got nothing as is yours.'

'Information,' Squeaky replied. 'Then we'll call the debt paid.'

'I got none! I ...' Then he looked at Squeaky's face and thought better of it. 'What?'

'House on Collins Street, number twenty-four.'

'What about it? It's not for sale.'

'Two men and a woman. Who are they?'

'Dunno. She's no use to you. She's not a working girl. Dunno what she is. Con artist of some sort. Got a nasty temper on her. Seen her spitting like a cat in a bucket of water.'

'They hurt her?'

The man's eyebrows shot up. ''Ow in 'ell do I know? Probably. She looked for it, an' all.'

'They new around here?'

'She is. They ain't.'

'But she's here because she wants to be?'

'Well, she ain't chained up! She may not like it, but she knows which side her bread's buttered.'

'Right. If that turns out to be true, you don't owe me any more.'

'Watch out for those two. Younger one's violent, but the old man's a right sod. Stick a knife in your back, quick as look at you.'

'Yeah? Well, I can be nasty too,' Squeaky said, although it was actually a long time since he'd even thought of such a thing. Respectable men in business didn't carry knives. More's the pity. 'I'll be back, if you're wrong!' he threatened at the doorway.

The man swore at him, but very half-heartedly, more out of habit than intent.

Worm was waiting on the pavement. 'What?' he said immediately.

Squeaky had known he would. It gave him no chance to think what he was going to say. If he embarked on a lie, he would have to follow it all the way. Worm had an awkwardly good memory, and

Squeaky was irritatingly unwilling to be caught in a lie. It would only be a lie to protect Worm from a truth he could not possibly understand yet. He did not want him even to imagine what the woman he thought was a lady would do to earn herself a meal and a roof over her head.

Why did the wretched child have to see moonbeams where there weren't any? Fairies on Christmas trees, shepherds and angels, and magical babies? It was all asking for trouble.

'She's there with them because she has to be,' he said tartly. 'She don't like them, and they don't like her, but sometimes there's no way round it.'

Worm said nothing for a moment or two. Then: 'We going back now to have a look?'

Squeaky was caught – again. Better to get it over with. Bad things put off only get worse. How was he going to explain it to the child? Simply. The more complicated it got, the more Worm would be convinced he was lying. Why did the damn woman have to look so innocent? It was probably her stock in trade. Damn her! What she did to men was her own affair, but not what she did to a child. Especially one Squeaky was supposed to look after.

'Are we?' Worm persisted.

'Yes, but you might not like what you see,' Squeaky replied, hating himself for having to say so; hating the men who treated women that way, the more so because he had been one of them, and he knew he had had a choice, which was more than a lot of women had; and hating this particular woman most of all because Worm cared. She had made him think better of her, and that was close to unforgivable. It was a deep sin to ignite dreams in a child that you could not live up to.

He knew perfectly well that she had not done it on purpose, but right now that did not justify anything. It made it worse, because she would walk away and leave Squeaky to mend the pieces. Damn her!

'Come on, then!' Squeaky said. He leaned forward, as if to take Worm's hand, then realised how ridiculous that was and scratched his leg instead.

They walked quickly but silently until they came back to a place just opposite the house where the lady – he still thought of her as that, to distinguish her from other women he knew – had gone inside willingly with the two men.

'What do we do now?' Worm asked.

'You wait here,' Squeaky told him. 'I'm going on to see if there's anyone in. No point in standing here

56

in the freezing wind for an hour, if there isn't.' And before Worm could argue, he set off.

This time luck was with him – or not – and he had no choice. When he knocked, the lady opened the door. Squeaky found himself standing there, feet away from her, and no fancy windows to blur his view. Or her view of him: a tall, very thin man in a very old black frock coat and a black hat jamming down much of his very long, scruffy white hair.

Closer to, she was young, perhaps twenty-three or -four. Her skin was as fair and clear as if she had lived in the country, not one of the dirtiest cities in the world. Her hair was light brown, and the momentary shaft of sunlight showed golden glints in it. Her features were pleasing, and unmarked by any petulance or ill temper.

'Are there any gentlemen at home?' Squeaky asked with an uncharacteristically uncertain voice.

'No, I'm sorry. Did you wish to see them?' She looked at him with dark blue eyes that were unusually penetrating.

He would not care to try lying to her. He had a feeling she knew lies well enough to spot one before it was even finished. She was probably very good at telling them herself.

Squeaky decided the whole truth was probably the best course. He waved his hand towards Worm, standing watching them from the opposite pavement. 'The boy saw you in the street yesterday, and was worried the men were a bit rough with you. Nothing would settle him but to see you are all right.' Without waiting for her answer, he signalled Worm to come over.

Worm did so immediately. The street was clear of traffic, and in a moment he was standing beside Squeaky. Now that the time was here, he was suddenly shy.

The lady looked at him and smiled slowly.

Worm smiled back. It irradiated his face, although it was a little lopsided, because one of his front teeth was bigger than the other. They were his first adult teeth fully through.

'My name is Eloise,' she said. 'What's yours?'

'Warren, but they call me Worm.'

'Then I shall call you Worm as well.'

He smiled, a little awed. He was standing so close that Squeaky could feel a slight pressure against his leg. Suddenly, he was intensely defensive of this nuisance child, but he had no idea what to do about it.

Eloise spoke. 'I understand you were afraid the men had taken me against my will. I saw you there in the street, just for a moment.' She smiled very slightly. 'I don't like them very much, but I did come with them willingly. Because I need to.'

Worm leaned even closer to Squeaky and said nothing.

Eloise stepped back. 'It's freezing in the wind out there. Come in. See that I'm all right.' She pulled the door wide open.

Squeaky hesitated. Why had she invited them in? Were the two men really somewhere else? He had nothing worth stealing. He knew better than to go walking in the streets of areas like this, carrying more than a few pence, enough for a meal. Not that he couldn't feel a pickpocket before he drew a second breath. But he was concerned about what else she was going to say to Worm.

Worm was ahead of him, following her, when she turned to lead the way.

Squeaky closed the door. She was right about one thing: it was perishing cold outside and beginning to rain.

Inside the house was warm, but dirty. She led the way into the kitchen, where the stove was lit. Squeaky glanced around quickly. It was very sparsely furnished. Just a few pots and pans, plates, enough for three on the old wooden dresser. There was a sink in the corner, so at least there was running water. But it was all so grubby, as if people had lived here for weeks, or even months, without ever scrubbing the floor or the surfaces of table and benches. There was a bowl of water on the table now, and a scrubbing brush beside it, next to a bar of yellow kitchen soap smelling of carbolic.

'We interrupted you,' Squeaky observed.

Eloise smiled ruefully. 'Just moved in. Hasn't been done for weeks. It'll look a lot better when I've finished.'

Squeaky had no idea whether to believe her or not. Perhaps it didn't matter.

Worm looked around. 'You really like it here?' he asked.

Eloise smiled and it was full of regret. It made her face suddenly softer, more vulnerable.

Worm saw it, although he would not have known what to call it. 'You don't have to stay. We can take you away, Squeaky and me. We have a place that's clean and dry … and warm. You can stay there.' He looked up at Squeaky. 'Can't she?'

What on earth could he say? He was caught again. What would Claudine say? He was being ridiculous. The place was full of prostitutes. That was what it was for – to help sick and injured women of the street. What was one more or less?

'Course,' he said between his teeth. 'But she said she's all right.'

'I am,' Eloise repeated, but she didn't sound so certain.

'You'd be safe,' Worm went on.

A shadow crossed her face. 'I'm safe here.'

Squeaky knew that was a lie, but it was one she wished them to believe. This was more complicated than he had thought. What had they stepped into?

'Really,' she assured them. 'And it will clean up quite well. After a fourth or fifth scrub, anyway. It's not for ever.'

'Where will you go then?' Worm asked.

'None of our concern!' Squeaky said sharply, cutting him off before he could say any more. 'She's all right. She said so.'

There was a moment's silence, anything but comfortable.

'You like them?' Worm asked Eloise.

'No,' she said, then immediately seemed to regret

it. 'Not ... not very much. But sometimes we have to put up with people we don't like a lot.' Her lip curled as if she smelled something unpleasant. Then she saw recognition of it in Worm's face. She seemed to struggle with something: dislike, temptation, indecision. 'I need to do it,' she said quietly, anger in her face now. 'Please ... just ... thank you, but I am where I wish to be. It was kind of you, but please go now.' The darkness came back into her face. 'I don't want to have to explain to them that you thought I was ... in danger. They will think I have been speaking about them behind their backs.'

Worm looked crushed.

'Go!' she repeated. She turned to Squeaky. 'Mr ...?'

'Robinson,' he supplied.

'Mr Robinson. Please don't come back.' Now her voice was cold, and there was a definite edge to it.

Worm did not move.

Squeaky tried one more time. 'Are you sure?'

Before she could answer, the door at the front slammed loudly and there were footsteps in the passage, at least two sets, heavy and determined. The inner door flew open and the older man stood in the entrance, the younger one on his heels.

'Oh, yes? And who are you?' the older man asked

Squeaky. He did not seem at first even to see Worm.

'They were just going,' Eloise said quickly, her voice full of apology.

The man remained blocking the doorway. 'Oh, yeah? And why are you here at all, eh?'

'I was enquiring for a friend of mine who keeps a shop around here,' Squeaky said, a sharp edge to his voice. He hoped the man recognised it for anger and did not take it as fear.

'In my kitchen?' the older man said. 'Likely … and all!' He made as if he were going to spit, and then changed his mind.

'It's cold outside,' Squeaky said with a smile, a challenging one, a baring of the teeth.

'Who?'

'Wally Jones.' He was a pimp Squeaky had known several years ago, but he was probably still alive … somewhere.

'Never heard of him. Now scarper!' the younger man said. 'Do you hear me?'

'That right?' the older man asked Eloise roughly. 'You better be telling the truth. You lie and I'll make you wish you'd never been born.'

'Then you'll never know what I know, will you?' she flashed back instantly.

He lifted his hand as if to strike her.

Worm lunged forward, as if he could do something.

Squeaky dived after him and caught him by the scruff of his collar, bringing him to the ground.

Eloise snatched at a pan from the top of the stove and hit the older man with it hard, not on the head, but on the shoulder. He howled with pain and screamed at her.

The younger man came forward, looked at Eloise with the pan, and stayed out of her reach.

Worm climbed to his feet.

'I don't need your help,' Eloise said, addressing Squeaky, but still keeping an eye on both of the other men.

'They'll kill you!' Squeaky protested.

'No, they won't,' she said with conviction. 'They want something I've got, something my father told me about, and they won't hurt me until I've given it to them.'

'And then what?' Squeaky said derisively. 'They're going to let you leave?' His total disbelief was heavy in his voice.

'Now listen here,' began the older man. 'This has nothing to do with you. It's between us and the woman.'

'Yes,' Eloise said, calmly answering Squeaky as if the other man hadn't spoken. 'I'll tell them where it is, and by the time they get it, I'll be long gone.'

'That's what you think,' snapped the younger man.

'I don't trust them and I'm not stupid. Now get out before this gets ugly,' Eloise told Squeaky.

It was well past ugly in Squeaky's mind. 'Come on.' He put his hand on Worm's shoulder, gripping his hand. 'We have to go.'

Worm resisted him for a moment, then could see that it was no use and gave in.

They went back along the dirty passage and to the door on to the street again. The wind had risen, and was even colder, but it was not yet properly raining. Squeaky found himself shivering as they started to walk along the street towards the main road, where they could catch an omnibus west again.

For a long time Worm did not say anything. He was turning what had happened over and over in his mind, trying to get it right. It couldn't be the way it seemed, could it? She wanted to stay in that drab, dirty house with those men? No, she had to. Why? She belonged somewhere clean and light, and warm all through. He and Squeaky would have taken her to the clinic. She would have been safe there, because

65

everybody was. And she would have had enough to eat, every day!

She looked so different from the women who usually came to the clinic, the sort of person who would never be with men like that, if she didn't have to. They were cruel. It was in their faces, and in what they said, and in the way they said it. He tried to remember, and was certain that she was frightened. Why would you stay with people that frightened you, if you didn't have to?

Had Squeaky taken him away because he was frightened they would hurt him – Worm? Or both of them?

'Is that why you went?' he said.

'Is what?' Squeaky might have known what Worm was talking about, but he wasn't going to admit it.

'In case they hurt us?' Worm said patiently.

'She doesn't want to leave them, Worm. You've got to face that. She's there because she wants to be. She don't have to explain it to us. Who are we? Two people she doesn't know who saw her in the street and got the wrong end of the stick.'

Worm looked at Squeaky's face and saw a shadow of sadness in it, as if he, too, had wanted it to be different. Why would he not admit it? Did he think that Worm would think he was silly?

66

No, of course not. Squeaky wouldn't care what Worm thought of him. Why should either of them feel sad because Eloise did not need them?

'Are you going to get Christmas stuff?' he asked. If Squeaky wanted to do it, then perhaps they should.

Squeaky looked straight ahead of them and kept walking. 'Yes, I know where we can get some red ribbons. And cheap. Might get some other things, too.'

'What things?'

'All kinds of things. Be quiet, and save your breath for walking!'

Worm fell silent. Squeaky was feeling bad, too, sort of ... disappointed. It was as if they were going to give Eloise a present, and she didn't want it.

*

The next morning, Squeaky had bookkeeping to do with all the papers in his office, and Worm was glad because every time he looked at Squeaky he thought of Eloise, and those two men he was still sure she was frightened of. He should do something else. Think of something else. Claudine had already been out and bought the two geese they were going to eat, and they were hanging in the pantry. With four days to go until Christmas there were lots of nice things in there: currants and spices, lots of butter and sugar and flour, and something that looked like bits of orange peel, all covered with tiny crystals of sugar. And more sugar, and brown sugar, and syrup, golden syrup. And other things, too, in brown paper bags. She had told him he would be in everlasting trouble if he touched any of them. They were standing in the kitchen when she said it. She was smiling, but she looked as if she really meant it. Worm was pretty good at telling when people meant what they said.

She looked at him a moment or two longer. 'You're very quiet, Worm. Are you all right?'

He wanted to say that, no, he wasn't. He felt hollow and lonely inside. He had thought for a moment he could really help the lady with the sun in her hair, but she had turned out to be an ordinary woman who actually wanted to be with the horrible men who had taken her in the first place, when Worm had seen her reluctant and frightened. They were dirty men. Outside dirt you couldn't help, but inside was different. That was your own fault.

She had not wanted either Worm or Squeaky to help her. But he was nine years old. Didn't matter. He was far too big to cry over something like that.

He looked up at Claudine. 'Yeah. I'm fine,' he replied. 'Are you going to like Christmas?' She should smile and say yes to that. Squeaky said everybody liked Christmas, but especially women, because they got to do all the preparing. Worm was not sure that women liked preparing all that much. It was pretty well what they did every day. That, and clean and clear away, and clean again.

Claudine looked at him closely. 'I will like Christmas very much, if everyone else does. Christmas is not a good time to be alone. We must make sure everybody is included.'

Funny, that was more or less what Squeaky had said, but Worm was not certain Claudine would like it if he told her so. He had made a few mistakes like that. There was sometimes a sadness inside Claudine, too, although she never said so. 'I'll help you,' he said instead.

'That would be very nice, thank you,' she accepted. 'We'll start by putting up some of these ribbons Squeaky got for us. For heaven's sake, he got enough for us to tie up the whole house.'

Worm did not really understand, but she seemed to be pleased, so he smiled as well.

*

69

It was the middle of the afternoon before they finished. Claudine made the most beautiful bows, with big, fat bright top pieces and long trailing ends. Every one was even, and the ribbon was shiny. Then she and Worm had fun deciding where to put them.

*

It was three o'clock, and not so long before it would get dark, when Worm finally excused himself. He had an idea. He had seen how Claudine liked the ribbons, and how red especially made her smile. He had several pennies he had saved up, a bit here, a bit there. Some of it was in ha'pennies and farthings, but it was still money. He would go and buy her a present. Now that they had put up the ribbons, he knew what he was going to get for her, and also how and where to find it.

Once, for a very short time, he had worked for a kidsman. And he had had the fright of his life. Kidsmen taught small children how to steal things, like silk handkerchiefs, sometimes lace ones. They were so light, people did not feel them go, if it was done right. Worm knew how to do it right, but once he had been caught, picked up like a little animal and shaken until his teeth rattled.

70

Someone had misunderstood and thought he was being wrongly beaten, and in the ensuing tussle he had escaped and never gone back to that street, or to that kidsman.

But he knew where to find him. He would not steal anything for Claudine. Even if she never knew, Worm would know, and that was enough. But if he could find the kidsman, he would buy a kerchief or a fichu for Claudine, one that she would really like. And he would know he had bought it with his own money. She would know he was telling the truth, because she always knew.

First, he must find the kidsman. He had a special area he used to work, down Mile End way. It was the area Worm had grown up in, and he knew a bit about it. That was not very far from where Eloise had gone, but there were thousands of people around there, and Worm knew how not to be noticed, especially in the shadows of late afternoon and early evening.

He would take an omnibus there. It was too far to walk and get there before the day was really dark. The fare would cost a little bit of his money, but there was no help for it.

He was lucky with buses, but it still was more

than an hour later, and definitely completely dark, when he got to Mile End. Worm went to Old Montague Street, running the same way as the Whitechapel Road, but a block further away from the river. He was looking for Pockets George. He knew George was still around, and he remembered where he lived. This was one of the shortest days of the year, and dark, but not too cold. George might be out and about, but more likely he would come home soon. He was called Pockets because he used to be one of the best pickpockets in London before the rheumatism got to him and he started using children to do the work for him.

He would be getting well organised before Christmas now, before a real cold snap came. 'Days get longer, weather gets stronger,' he used to say. And it was true. Weather got worse after the shortest day. If it was going to be ice, black ice you couldn't see and people slipped on – sometimes even buses did, and whole carts would go over – then most people stayed in. Wasn't a good time to pick silk handkerchiefs. People kept their hands in their pockets.

The streetlamps were lit now. Worm liked street-lamps; he liked the shape of them. They would have been a square, except they were bigger at the top, much bigger, and they had an extra piece on the very top. They had a yellow light, as if it were warm. If it was foggy, they had a ring of light around them.

There were still lots of people about, even on Old Montague Street. He walked along, staying in the shadows, with his hands in his pockets to keep them warm. It took him a few attempts before he got the right place, then he knocked on the door. He thought Pockets must be at home because there was smoke coming out of the chimney. He could just see it in the wisps where it crossed the light of the nearest streetlamp.

Pockets came to the door. 'Yes?' he said, squinting a little to make out who it was.

'Worm,' Worm said. 'I come to buy something.'

'Ha! You got money?'

'Course I have,' Worm said indignantly.

''Ow much?'

Worm had been caught that way before. 'Show me what you got. You always have the best hankies, an' such.'

'And since when did you want a fine handkerchief?'

'Since I've got to give something to a nice lady

wot gives me Christmas dinner and a nice place to sleep.'

'Oh! Indeed! Then I'd better be sure you don't give her back one of her own, hadn't I?' Pocket said with a sneer.

Worm began to feel uncomfortable. This wasn't working out the way he had meant it to. 'Ain't you got none, then?' he challenged.

'I 'ave. Come in and see.' Pockets turned and led the way to another room, where there were three chests of drawers. 'How old is this lady?'

'Middling old. Not very,' Worm replied.

'Grey hair?'

'No. Not that old.'

Pockets considered for a moment. He was clearly thinking hard. ''Ow 'bout this?' he said eventually. 'It's the prettiest I got.' He opened one drawer a bit, and pulled out a long silk scarf that was so light it seemed to float in the air. It was soft, and all made of pinks and reds and golds. As he let it drift to the ground, Worm could see it was actually pictures of roses, big ones with dozens and dozens of petals, all just about melting into each other. It was the most beautiful thing he had ever seen. He bent to touch it, and was not sure whether he really did or not, it was so soft.

'Like it?' Pockets asked gently, his voice mimicking the touch of the silk.

Worm did not even look at him. He knew something dreadful was coming. Pockets never gave anything for less than he could get for it. The scarf was probably worth gold.

There was no point in lying. Pockets would see right through that. As if anyone would not like it. In his imagination, Worm could already see Claudine's face when she saw it.

'I haven't got that much money,' he said.

'I can give you a cheaper one.' He did not mean *give,* he still meant *sell.* He brought another out of the drawer. If Worm had not seen the roses, he would have thought it good. But not now. He couldn't give that to Claudine with any pleasure. She would say she liked it, but he would always know how she would have liked the roses, as he had. And Pockets knew it, too.

'So?' Pockets said. 'Which one do you want, then? I can give you the second one, for … say … one shilling and sixpence. The first one is worth a lot more, twenty times as much.'

Worm stared at him. 'I ain't stealing.'

'Nobody asked you to steal. You're not that good

at it, anyway. You'd only get caught, and that's no use to anyone. I want you to go on an errand for me, then I'll give you the scarf for payment?'

'When I've run the errand, how do I know you'll give me the scarf?'

'Getting smart, aren't you! 'Cos you don't tell me what I want to know till I do give you the scarf. If you don't tell me then, you know what I'll do to you.'

Worm shivered. It was as good a bargain as he was going to get. He accepted. 'A'right, what do I have to do?'

Pockets described to him exactly the place he was to go, a small, crowded, dirty public house less than half a mile away. There he was to wait until two men came, separately, and fell into conversation. One of them was very easy to recognise. He was called Ginger, because he had a mass of ginger-coloured hair, and a beard to match. In the summer, you could see the ginger hair on his arms, but at this time of year he favoured a ragged peacoat that was once navy blue, and now had no particular colour at all.

'Then what?' Worm asked.

'He's going to meet a woman I know called Pie,

'cos she always looks like she's drunk – pie-eyed – except she's as sober as a judge, underneath it. And Pie's going to ask him some questions, and bring me back the answers. Only Pie is going to lie to me, and I want you to listen real hard and bring me back the truth. If you do, the scarf with the roses is yours. If you don't, I'll put you in the river with the scarf tied around your neck. Then everyone'll say I strangled you with a scarf o' roses. Understand?'

Worm swallowed hard and nodded.

'And if you just run off, I'll find you. London ain't big enough to hide in. Not any part as you can find, anyway. Get it?'

'Then you'll give me the roses? I got friends, too. What are very nice if they like you, but take it real rotten if you tread on them, on their toes.'

'Oh, yeah? And are you one of them toes, like?'

'Yes, I am!' Worm raised his eyes and looked at Pockets squarely. He was surprised to see amusement there, rather than anger.

'Right. Don't stand there like a weed growing out of the floor. Get going!' Pockets replied.

Worm did as he was told. The prize of the scarf with roses was worth working for. He found the public house easily enough and stepped inside without anyone bothering him. He could pretend he was hungry, actually not much of a pretence needed, and would collect dirty glasses and carry them to the kitchen for a sandwich later on.

It was half an hour before he saw the big man with the mass of ginger hair. He would have been hard to miss. It wasn't long after that when a woman, apparently drunk, staggered up and sat down in the chair next to him.

Worm made himself as small as possible. He must remember every word he heard. The scarf with the roses depended on it.

*

When he got back to Pockets, it was far later than he had meant to be out. They would be wondering where he was at the clinic. He might catch the rough side of Squeaky's tongue, although Squeaky would lie to Claudine, not to defend Worm, but to stop her from worrying.

'Well?' Pockets demanded as soon as Worm was through the door. There was no 'Are you all right?' No hot cup of tea.

'They came.' Worm tried to concentrate and think

of nothing else except what he had heard, before he had forgotten any of it. 'Ginger was there, and after a few minutes Pie came in. She was falling over on her feet, until she sat down. But when she spoke, she was like you said, sober as a judge.'

'Yes! Yes, so what did she say?' Pockets demanded.

'She thought as they'd got the woman, but not sure it was going to do them any good. Wildcat she was, purring one minute and scratching their eyes out the next—'

'I don't care about that,' Pockets cut across him. 'Go on. Go on! What else?'

'It was about a robbery.' Worm was trying to keep it all straight in his mind. 'Lot of gold, but none of them know where it is now. Where's my scarf?'

'Yes, what? Oh.' Pockets pulled it from inside his coat. 'There! Now what else? Where's the old man … the one that took the loot?'

'He's dead, at least Ginger says he is.'

'C'mon, get on with it or I'll tie that scarf around your neck and pull it tight!'

'They chased him and he fell into the river. They think he drownded.'

'Are you sure?'

'That's what he said.'

'So what are they gonna do about it? Come on! They must've said something!'

'Yeah. They're going to get the truth out of the woman with the temper about where the old man, who's her father, hid the gold. They reckon as she knows.'

'They got her, then?'

'Yeah.'

'Where?'

'They never said.'

'Are you sure? Think hard.'

'Somewhere not far, but they didn't say. That's the truth. Can I go now? It'll take me an hour to get back, and they'll skin me for being out so late.'

Pockets looked reluctant. 'Then I suppose you expect me to cough up the fair for a hansom to carry you back and all?'

'Yeah? I mean –' he hesitated a moment – 'yeah.'

Pockets fished in his coat and brought out a shilling. 'Cab fare, mind, no going out and buying 'am sandwiches!'

'Cab fare, promise.'

'Go on then, get out!'

*

It seemed like a long cab ride back to Portpool Lane, but it was over far too quickly, and exactly as Worm had expected, he was barely inside the back kitchen door when Squeaky's bony hand descended on his shoulder.

Worm jumped. He had been half expecting it, but it still caught him by surprise. 'Ow!'

'That all you've got to say for yourself?' Squeaky said softly, which was more frightening than if he had shouted.

'No ...'

'What, then? I lied to Miss Claudine for you. You'd better have a very good answer, or I'll tell her the truth.'

'No, you won't.' Worm wriggled hard, but could not get free. 'You lied so she wouldn't worry, for her, not for me.' He realised he was taking a great risk. Maybe too much. 'I've got a present for her, but I had to earn it. Let me go, and I'll show you.'

'Earn it? How?' Squeaky said suspiciously.

'Go on an errand. Let go of me and I'll show you.'

Squeaky let go.

Worm shook himself and then fished inside his jacket, then inside his shirt, and pulled out the scarf. Even in the one light left on in the kitchen all night,

it still looked magically beautiful. He looked into
Squeaky's eyes, waiting for approval. It mattered a
lot.

'Where'd you get that?' Squeaky said in amazement. He put out one finger to touch it and felt its
softness. 'Where'd you get it?'

'You think she'll like it?' Worm asked.

Squeaky breathed out slowly. 'Yes. It'll be the most
beautiful scarf she's ever seen. Now where the hell
did you get it?'

Worm grinned. 'I ran an errand, and I earned it. I
didn't take it!'

'Never thought you had,' Squeaky lied. 'Give it
me. I'll put it somewhere safe, like with the money.
We'll have to find some piece of paper and wrap it
up.' His eyes narrowed. 'Now what? Worm! This
errand – tell me about it.'

'I … in the morning.'

'Now! Want a cup of tea?'

'Yes.'

'And a piece of fruitcake?'

'Yes.'

Ten minutes later they sat at the kitchen table in
a pool of light, mugs of tea before them, and two
large slices of cake.

They ate in silence for several minutes. The tea was too hot to drink straight away. Finally, Squeaky spoke. 'What's wrong, then?'

Worm considered saying that nothing was wrong, but Squeaky always knew a lie when he heard it. Perhaps he had told so many himself he could know from the moment you started. And Worm did want to tell someone.

Squeaky waited. He tried his tea, but it was still too hot. He cut another slice of cake for each of them. It was very good, moist in the middle, nothing was dried out and hard He would have to consider some way to explain its absence in the morning.

'I had a story to remember, and get exact,' Worm began, his mouth full of cake. Then he stopped.

'So, what was it?' Squeaky asked.

Worm swallowed. 'There was a robbery. Two men, and one older. The older man took the loot, they don't know where. The only person who might know is a woman – with a terrible temper. But they killed the man, or they think they did.' His eyes never left Squeaky's face.

Squeaky's mind raced. He knew now what Worm was afraid of. 'You see any of these people?' he asked, more to give himself a moment to think than because he expected any useful answer.

'Just the man and the woman what was talking.' Hope flickered in Worm's eyes, but already Squeaky had an answer. 'They're called Ginger, because he has ginger hair, and Pie 'cos she's always pie-eyed.' He said it with a lift in his voice, as if he thought it might help.

'Any other name?' Squeaky asked.

'No.'

'What're you thinking?' Squeaky did not wait for an answer. 'It's a big imagine from that to Eloise. That's what you're thinking, isn't it?'

'Is it?' Worm asked earnestly. 'They said they got the young woman – and with a temper – and they think they killed her father, but they dunno where the gold is, and she does.'

Squeaky's mind raced. He really badly did not want this to be true. 'Could be,' he agreed. 'Or fifty others.' He looked at the hope and the fear in Worm's face. Could he lie to him, to ease his fear? If it were Eloise, then she was in bad trouble. It would explain why the two men, the older one and the younger, wished so much to keep her. It didn't explain why she went with them. He pointed that out to Worm.

'Yeah, it does,' Worm said very quietly. 'If they killed the old man, and he were her father, she'd want to get back at them for it.'

Squeaky had to think of an alternative. 'Well, maybe she wants the money, too, and thinks *they* know where it is,' he pointed out. And then instantly he regretted it. Which was worse, that she was a victim and might end up dead? Or that she was going to try to kill one, or both of them, in revenge for her father's death? Either way, they could not help her, and Worm would suffer knowing that.

What kind of story would make it all right?

Worm was watching, and waiting for him to say something.

Squeaky's mind slid back to a time and a place he had never meant to go again. Once, when he was young, and more than a little awkward, a woman he had admired had been in difficulties. He had hesitated and his courage had failed him. She preferred someone else, he was certain of that, and he had stood aside rather than risk being rebuffed. She had been hurt in both emotion and reputation. He could have persisted, or at least he could have tried. He still remembered it with regret. How different would his life have been if he had tried? Better? Worse?

He would never know. Memory remained, always touched with guilt.

Now here he was, trying to protect Worm, the same way he had protected himself, and never known what he had lost. Better to hurt for trying and failing, than hurt for not trying.

He plunged in. 'We should think hard, and then make a plan.'

Immediately Worm sat up a little straighter, his eyes bright.

Squeaky felt his throat tighten until he could hardly breathe. Had he lost his wits? After a lifetime of playing it safe, always thinking before he acted, always knowing the way to escape, if need be, here he was rushing into something he had absolutely no need to even think about! Let alone do.

'What?' Worm prompted. 'What should we do?'

Squeaky chose his words very carefully. 'First, we have to know as much as we can, and know it right, not just guessing.'

'I'll come with you,' Worm said immediately.

'No, you won't! They'll remember us if we're together. I'll dress different, so's even you wouldn't know me.'

Worm looked sceptical, but he didn't argue.

'And anyway, there are things to do here. You're to help Miss Claudine with Christmas ...'

'I don't know ...'

'Just do as you're told! Tie ribbons, climb up ladders, fetch and carry stuff. Tell her stories about where I've gone, if you have to.'

Worm bit his lip. 'She knows when I'm lying.'

'You won't be lying. You'll just be repeating what I tell you. Don't argue, or we'll be here all night. Drink your tea, and listen. We've got to tidy up, get rid of those cake crumbs.'

'They'll know,' Worm pointed out. 'Half the cake is gone.'

Squeaky looked at it. 'Not quite half, but near as made no difference. Well, there's one thing I've got to do – fetch more stuff for making cakes.'

'What can I do?'

'Whatever she tells you, so she's so busy looking after you, she won't wonder where I am!' Squeaky told him. 'Now go to bed!'

*

But Squeaky did not sleep well, even though he was tired. What had he got himself into? He was probably

87

going to discover that Eloise and her father were thieves, and that he had been killed when they tried to take all of the money, instead of sharing it. The whole story would end in a squalid mess. Poor Worm, and his lady with the light in her hair.

Could Squeaky make up something that sounded better? Almost anything was better than that.

Except that Worm smelled a lie as quickly as Claudine did, so then he would have lost Squeaky as someone he could trust. It would hurt him very much indeed. More than a lost dream of Eloise? Perhaps, because it was a real loss.

Was it? Squeaky was no one's ideal of anything. Why did he care so much what Worm thought of him? It was ridiculous. Perhaps it was better anyway if Worm realised Squeaky was a scoundrel, and sometimes a thief. Or used to be! He was still a good forger, when needs must. Respectable on the outside now, but it was only as thick as a coat of paint.

You could make beautiful pictures with paint, but there was nothing behind it.

He lay in the dark and stared at the ceiling he could not see. Did anybody really change? Could he be what Worm thought he was?

And what was that? Apart from someone who didn't lie to him.

What was the truth about Eloise, anyway? Perhaps he should begin by finding out. He would decide what to say when he knew what the reality was. A good lie had to have some element of truth in it, if possible.

*

He began in the morning, as soon as his urgent chores were done. As usual, they were matters of money: what they could afford to restock in their supplies of medicine, bandages, bedlinen, and food suitable for invalids recovering from fevers, injuries, or just the effects of being outside in the London winter. No doubt every bed in the whole of these two and a half houses joined together would be occupied. Why should someone be outside and alone at Christmas? It was even possible, if the night were wet, or freezing, that they might have people asleep on the floor at the entrance hall. They had done last year.

And food! There was certainly no limit to the amount a hungry urchin like Worm would eat! It didn't have to be stuffed goose and Christmas pudding; it could be a heel of stale bread and a little jam. Good thing Claudine supervised the making of barrel-loads of jam in the season when you could buy a cartful of plums, a little overripe, for a few shillings. And rhubarb. Who would've thought that rhubarb would make such nice jam? He had seen her put a little ginger in it. Perhaps that was what made the difference. She had a good hand at certain things, for a woman who had a cook at home, and never even went into her own kitchen.

He was avoiding the issue. The books were all balanced. He had accomplished jobs he had been putting off for weeks. There was nothing left to keep him at Portpool Lane. He found his oldest coat and a hat with a crumpled brim, just the look of which made him appear drunk. He put them on, and went out into the wind and the rain.

He began by looking up a few old acquaintances and asking casual questions. He learned very little. He didn't know the names of the two men who had taken Eloise, although he could describe them well enough to learn that the older was called Oldham. Easy enough to remember. The younger was known by various nicknames, none of them memorable.

Apparently, the two were cousins and had practised their thieving and various other skills for years. Squeaky was happy to call the second man Younger. Both had served time in the Cold Bath Fields prison. They must be tough to have survived that, and come out alive. Not that many did.

That was instructive, but not good news. It put the whole issue in rather a different league from the petty theft he had supposed. This was bad.

Squeaky sat in a café over a cold cup of tea and thought about it, putting off the decision. He had a suspicion what robbery it was all about. It had been recounted in the newspapers. He argued with himself for over half an hour why it was not that robbery, but some other. And if it was, it was far better he leave the whole matter alone.

Yet he knew this kind of people. A picture of Goldie came to his mind, as she used to be, way back. It was not one he wanted, but he could never completely shake it from his mind. It was woven through everything else he would prefer to forget. He was a different person now. For a start, he was thirty years older! Thirty hard years, full of events he was not proud of. He had thought them all right at the time: clever, necessary for survival in the hard

91

world to which he belonged. But looked back on now, too many of them were shabby.

But he knew Goldie was still alive. He heard news of her every so often, though he tried to avoid it.

No. That was a lie. Sometimes he tried to avoid it. Sometimes, like any other old wound, it came back in a surprising echo, when he passed a place they had been together, quarrelling as usual. Or someone mentioned a name from the past, usually these days saying that they were dead. Always he pretended not to care. And always he did.

Regret? Not really. Not now. He would much rather not know how she had changed with time. It probably wasn't good. Her temper would be even worse with hard times, and growing old. She could be spiteful. She was beginning to fade even then.

But the longer he stared at the cold tea, the more he knew that he would have to go and find her in the end. She was the one source of the kind of information he would need if he was going to help Eloise get free of the two men who had killed her father.

He put it off a little longer. There were more things to find out first. He stood up slowly and went out into the street. It had stopped raining and the wind was blowing harder, colder. There were clear patches in the sky. Tonight it would certainly freeze.

There was a policeman who had made one or two mistakes of which Squeaky knew the details. He would be willing to help. It would be easy to see him and ask him.

Squeaky had exerted a little pressure as second nature in the past. Now he thought of what Claudine would think of him and was distinctly uncomfortable, which was ridiculous! She thought he was a disgusting old reprobate, who happened to be very clear-minded at keeping the books at the clinic, and finding supplies they needed at very reasonable prices indeed. And it was her Christian duty as a good woman not to remember his past too closely. And she *was* a good woman, a fact that both gave him pleasure and irritated him like salt in a cut. He wouldn't change it, even if he could. He did not want another Goldie, or anything like her. She belonged to the past.

He was familiar with the policeman's beat. It was a good piece of knowledge to have. Never knew when it might be useful.

He had to take an omnibus to make certain he was on time to catch Alf as he came off duty. As it was, he nearly missed him.

'Hello, Alf,' Squeaky said, catching up with him on the narrow footpath, as they turned the corner on to Tooley Street. Lamplight was momentarily bright, a little over to their right. Higher up the hill the train rattled by on its way to London Bridge station. Beneath them the wide spread of the river reflected the riding lights of the big ships glittering on the black water.

Alf froze, then turned around slowly. 'If you creep up on me again, you squint-eyed sod, I'll do you, I swear! I thought you'd died. I haven't heard from you for so long, I thought all my wishes had come true. What do you want?'

'Same as always,' Squeaky said, as if he hadn't even heard the insult. 'A little information. Not much, just want it quickly and without anyone knowing I'm interested.'

Alf was in no way reassured. 'What information?'

'About a robbery, two years ago. The loot was never found ...'

'It's never found in most of them,' Alf said witheringly. 'Why? You think you found it? Then you're a fool to tell me, 'cos I'll just turn you in.'

'More like you'll keep it yourself,' Squeaky rejoined immediately. 'Like before! Maybe you've conveniently forgotten. I haven't.'

Alf flushed a dull red. 'There were only a few bob!'

'I don't remember the details,' Squeaky said with a smile that should have turned Alf's blood cold if he could see it in the dusk. 'But I could – if I have to.'

'What robbery was it, then?' Alf asked, trying to smile back.

'Gold,' Squeaky replied. 'Three men, I think. Definitely two. An older one and a younger. Quarrelled. Think they might have killed the third.'

'Ah! That one. Yeah, I think they did. Stupid, as then they lost the loot. All that for nothing.' Alf said that with satisfaction.

'So tell me what you know,' Squeaky said. He could not turn back now, but he was not at all sure he really wanted to learn the details.

'That's it,' Alf protested, moving away a step.

Squeaky seized his arm. 'No, it isn't. Names. Dates. How much gold? Where from, and where did they run to?'

Alf looked at him. 'What's it worth?'

'Nineteen shillings and sixpence,' Squeaky said slowly and carefully. That was the exact sum Alfred had kept when he had should have handed it in – a policeman's wages for a week.

Alf paled. He said something under his breath, but Squeaky chose not to hear it. 'Truscott and Company,' Alf said reluctantly. 'Great Hermitage Street. Other side of the river.'

'I know where it is. When?'

'October the fifth. Two years ago. I don't know how much. Well over two thousand pounds worth. I could live nice for the rest of my life on that!'

'So could all of us,' Squeaky said with feeling. 'Which way did they go with it?'

'Towards the river. What else?'

'All three of them?'

'I don't know, and that's the truth.'

'Where does the woman come into it?'

'Woman? What woman?' Alf looked totally confused.

'What time of the day was it?'

'Dunno, 'bout three, I think. They got away and then it got dark, lost them. Don't know what happened. And that's all.' He jerked his arm away from Squeaky's grip.

Squeaky was inclined to believe him. He let it go. It was a lot more than he had had an hour before.

There was no alternative but to go back across the river to the north bank again and find Goldie. As if that would take much doing!

But was it worth it? What would he discover? That it was one more case of greedy people falling out over the spoils of a theft, hiding the haul, and then killing the one person who knew where it was? Now they were trying again to find it, with the daughter of the man they had murdered. It was both squalid and too easy to believe.

How could he make that any better for Worm? Should he leave it alone? It was bad enough, and he could only find worse.

What would they do with Eloise if she found the gold for them? Stupid question. If they had killed her father and she knew it, they would kill her. Too obvious.

Two hours later, Squeaky was outside the familiar door to the club on the north side of the river, in the small back street. Goldie still owned it, and she lived above. He was nervous. His collar was too tight. His boots pinched. He was neither the man he had been, not yet the one he wished to be.

Damn it!

He banged loudly on the door. He was about to do so a second time when it opened. A small woman stood just inside. At least, she was short, though she was not small in girth. She used to be generously

97

proportioned; now she was just fat. Her hair was a brassy gold that nature had never intended. Indeed, to judge by her dark eyes and beautifully dark brows, Nature had probably meant it to be black. In spite of the fact that she was at this moment not very surprised and not very pleased, she still had the remnants of the beauty that had once made her famous. It was there in the bones, and the shape of her brows.

There was sharp memory in her eyes. 'Who in hell are you, then?' she said angrily.

'Losing your memory, are you? Perhaps it's just as well. I'm willing to lose some of mine, if you like?' Squeaky responded.

'I don't care what you do!' she snapped. 'Just don't do it on my front step.'

'I wasn't going to.' He pushed her shoulders gently, and she was obliged to step back or lose her balance. He followed her in and kicked the door shut with his heel, but not hard, only sufficiently to allow them both to enter.

'And what do you want, after all this time?' she said bitterly.

'Information,' he replied. 'What else have I ever wanted?'

She laughed harshly. 'More than you were ever going to get!'

'Likely more than you have, Goldie. Not more than you once had.' He walked past her into the sitting room. He was startled by how little it had changed. A bit more shabby, perhaps. The lamps were all still the same: coloured glass in pinks and golds, flowers painted on them. Fringes that moved if you touched them. The same small tables with the barley-twist legs, and mirrors framed in gold, placed to give the illusion of far more space than there was. Illusion. How much to do with everything was an illusion? All memory, dreams and wishes.

How different really was he from Worm, with his silly ideas about Eloise?

Suddenly he was furious with Eloise, for being so much less than a child thought she was. For himself, he didn't care any more whether Goldie was anything, or nothing. He wasn't a child; perhaps he never had been. He couldn't remember. He didn't want to know.

'I want to find out about two thieves – Oldham and the younger one he worked with. Tell me about them, and the gold robbery two years ago, at Truscott and Co.'

She stood with her hands on her hips. 'Why do

you want to know? I don't know where the gold is and nor does anyone else.'

''Cos the only one who knows is dead, right?'

She was surprised, but she tried to hide it. Then, watching his face, she knew she had failed. She shrugged sharply.

'Tell me about those two,' he insisted.

She walked over to the couch she favoured, close to the fire, and sat down hard. She left him to find his own seat.

'Nasty,' she began. 'Because they're afraid, inside themselves. Badly afraid.'

Squeaky sat down very slowly. Nothing made a sound. No letting out of air from a cushion, no rattle or clang of springs, even though more than one of them was broken.

'Oldham?' She was not asking him, rather calling up memories in herself.

Squeaky knew it was for effect; she never forgot anything about people. Such knowledge was her stock in trade. It had been what she sold that made her different. Anything physical was thrown in, a fore-play, not the substance.

Squeaky waited.

'He wants to be somebody. He wants people to

recognise him, remember him, you know ... One of those people who only exist if other people know them. Leave him to himself, or pass him by without knowing him, and he's empty. No one there.'

Squeaky was beginning to get an idea: only the seed, nothing real yet. But he determined to remember what she had said. 'And what about the younger one? What is he afraid of?'

'No sense of direction,' she said thoughtfully, pushing her lower lip out in a gesture of distaste.

Squeaky was disappointed. 'Doesn't sound like much.'

She looked at him narrowly. 'Do you know where you are?'

'Course I do ... You mean he doesn't?'

'I mean he don't ... belong nowhere. And that's no use to you. That he has everything exact, that's part of what upset him so much about losing the loot. They did some kind of trick on him with the place they put the gold. Full of tricks, the whole lot of them.' She said it as if it were an affliction, like having lice.

'What whole lot?' he asked. 'There was an old one and a young one, and the old man that got killed. Who else?'

'Maybe got killed,' she corrected, her mouth

turning down at the corners. 'Maybe not. His daughter, Lizzie, or whatever she was called, she's a tricky one, too. One moment looks like a saint, next moment a tart, a minute after that, a good quiet little nothing as you wouldn't look at twice.'

'Eloise?'

'Maybe.' Goldie made a grimace of distaste. 'What kind of a name is that?'

The kind of name of someone you want to be, Squeaky thought. He said, 'I don't know. French, maybe?'

'She's as English as I am!' Goldie said in disgust. 'Puts on airs like she's some kind of lady, if you ask me.'

'As English as you are?' Squeaky said. Then as soon as he saw her face, he regretted it. 'Or me,' he added quickly.

She could read him like an open book. She always had. But before, he had been young, and his hunger for some idea of love had made a fool of him. He had looked in all the wrong places. Now friendship mattered more. He smiled back at her to let her know his armour was complete. 'So, she's anything she wants to be, as suits her. In other words, she's a woman. Got to survive, I suppose.'

'What's the matter with you?' Goldie said incredulously. 'You're getting old, and soft in the 'ead!'

'We all get old … at least the lucky ones do. Others die young.'

'We don't all get soft in the 'ead,' she pointed out.

'No. Your 'ead's still as hard as your heart.' Then again, he wished he had not said that. He was letting his thoughts out too easily. Perhaps he was getting soft in something! 'So, she's clever …'

'Course she's clever, you old fool! Too damn clever by half. She'll end up getting herself killed. You'll see.'

'It was gold, not treasury notes and such?'

'I already told you!'

'How long did the old man have it? How long after the robbery did he disappear?'

'Couple o' days. I don't know. What's it to you, anyway? Why have you really come here?' She looked at him narrowly, suspicious again.

Because a small boy had dreams that were really delusions … but Squeaky did not want her ever to find that out. It mattered too much. But at the same time, Worm must never think that Squeaky lied to him. That would be a disillusion too far. Life was full of realities that were hard to take. There had to be at least one person who never lied to you, no matter how painful the truth. But he couldn't say that to Goldie. Damn it, it was hard enough to say to himself!

'Looking to recall old times, I suppose,' he lied.

She saw through it straight away. Time had not been kind to her, and she knew it. And 'old times' had not been so good either. Squeaky was not the kind to sentimentalise anything.

He shrugged. 'All right. I'd like to have that gold. It must still be around somewhere.'

'Good luck, you silly old fool! It will cost someone else their life yet! See if it don't.'

Very reluctantly he rose to his feet. If he stayed, he was going to give away something that might matter. The less she knew of his business, the better. 'Bye, Goldie,' he said, going to the door.

*

He saw Worm at breakfast the following morning in the kitchen, with the other staff.

'Getting close to Christmas,' he said to nobody in particular.

Worm sat up a little straighter.

'Got more things to find,' Squeaky went on, quite casually. 'Got an idea where I might get some nice gold-coloured balls. Take Worm with me.' He thought of saying to carry them, but had a better idea. 'Always works to take a child with you.'

'You're a cynic!' Ruby, the kitchen maid, said.

'Squeaky's eyebrows shot up. 'Where'd you learn that word?'

'From Miss Claudine ... Mrs Burroughs,' she corrected herself quickly. She was not in a position to be taking such liberties.

Squeaky stood up. 'Too sharp by half,' he said to Ruby. 'Come on,' he added to Worm. 'Leave you here, you'd eat all day!'

Worm jumped to his feet. 'Where're we going?'

'To find Eloise,' Squeaky said quietly, although they were at the back door and well out of the earshot of the kitchen.

'Why? What are we going to do? She didn't want to come with us. She said so,' Worm pointed out.

'People don't always mean what they say,' Squeaky said a trifle sententiously. When he said 'people' he actually meant women. He opened the back door and went outside, Worm on his heels. It was a little milder today. Perhaps it would not snow for

105

Christmas after all. Squeaky had mixed feelings about that.

'What are we going to do?' Worm persisted.

Squeaky had been expecting the question. 'First thing, we're going to find Eloise. She may be in the same place, and she may not. Then we're going to ask her the truth about why she's staying with those two men, and what she means to do. If it's the gold from the robbery, which they can't find, or if it's to pay them back for her father.'

'And then what?'

'Depends on what she says.' He was going to have to make it up a bit from here on. 'We have to stop her trying to kill them, because they'll end up killing her.'

Worm grabbed his hand, pulling hard. 'We've got to save her! And she wouldn't kill them! She must want to prove as her father didn't double-cross them!' There was desperation in his voice.

Should Squeaky say they needed to consider that perhaps her father did double-cross them? Would Worm want her to face that? And perhaps in her heart Eloise knew that anyway, and it was the opposite she was trying to prove? To get rid of that demon of doubt was her real need. And she was so tense because she was afraid she was wrong? What would she do if she were? Would she ever accept it?

There was no way to know.

Everyone has to accept disillusion sometime. Hardly anyone was as good as you believed. He supposed that was what love was: accepting someone the way they were. But nine was not the age do that, and Christmas was not the time. Maybe the whole Christmas idea was an illusion? But too many people needed it to be real for anyone to hack pieces off it.

Worm was silent, walking as quickly as he could, skipping a step or two to keep up. But he would not forget and he'd keep on asking for an answer. Either that, or he'd come to the conclusion that Squeaky was going to lic to him, even if only by silence. Then all silences became lies, or could do.

'We'll ask her,' Squeaky said finally.

Worm seemed satisfied with that.

But finding Eloise was not so easy. They went back to the house where they had seen her before, but it appeared to be empty. The front room, from what they could see through the windows, looked vacant and dirty.

'She's not here,' Worm said miserably. 'She wouldn't leave it like that.'

'You're too used to luxury, you are!' Squeaky said, thinking of Claudine's insistence on sweeping and scrubbing all the time. She kept the clinic like a hospital, or what he supposed a hospital was like. But then it was a hospital, of sorts, now. 'I'm going round the back,' he added. 'Maybe she just wants people to think there's no one here.' He had not spoken to Worm about seeing Goldie, or anything that he had been told. He would rather Worm didn't know about that. There was no need. Squeaky did not really know why he had wanted it kept secret or, if he were even halfway honest, he did not want to admit it. The more he looked at it with hindsight, the less of it he liked.

'Come on!' he said sharply. 'Don't just stand there!'

He went all the way round to the back with Worm on his heels. They followed the alley behind the whole row of houses, and went up the paved path between the rubbish tip and the outhouse to the back door. There was a light on in the kitchen.

Squeaky glared at Worm and then opened the door and stepped in.

Eloise was standing in the middle of the floor, a mop in her hand and a bucket at her feet. She looked startled, for a moment afraid, and then she recognised him. She held the mop a little like a weapon, as if she would use it as a lance. It would have been effective at face height, sodden with dirty water.

'What do you want now?' she demanded.

Squeaky looked at the mop. 'Why don't you throw that dirty bucket of water down the drain and talk nicely? Worm here thinks you could use a bit of help. I asked questions here and there, of people I know. I reckon it's the Truscott robbery your father was accused of. Gold was never found, that right?'

She stood absolutely still, the mop still in her hands. 'What do you know about it?'

'Two men, maybe three,' Squeaky replied, pulling one of the hard-backed chairs out from under the table and pointing to a second for Worm to do the same. He sat down carefully. 'One of them your father?'

She eased the mop into the bucket and propped it against the wall. 'No. He was going to do it with them, then he changed his mind.'

Or that was what he told her, Squeaky thought. He said, 'So who took the gold in the end? They didn't, or they wouldn't be after you to tell them where it is. They think that you know.' He looked

straight at her. She was a pretty woman. Very pretty
in a quiet way. She had a face you could look at for
a long time and still find it good. She had no business
to be so attractive, but he would not look for the bad
in her, for Worm's sake.

She sat down slowly opposite them, on the other
side of the table. Suddenly she looked tired, and she
avoided Squeaky's eyes when she answered. 'They
talked him into it. I don't know how. He didn't need
the money, not that badly, though business was
hard—'

'What did he do?' Squeaky interrupted.

'He was a smith. Made things out of pewter. Jugs
and teapots and salt dishes. He could make really
beautiful stuff.' Her face had a soft, dreamy look, as
is she were seeing memories of lovely things created,
visions of the past that were happy.

Squeaky looked at Worm and then back at her
again. Perhaps her father really was an artist. And
perhaps not. Better pretend to believe it anyway.
'Sounds good. What went wrong?' he asked.

'A man commissioned a whole teapot set, hot-water
jug, milk jug, everything. Money he paid for it was
forged.' She looked on the edge of tears. Real tears?
Or self-pity. The story could be true. There was lots

of forged money around, from treasury notes through to threepenny bits. Must have been notes. An artist in metal surely wouldn't be fooled that easily by coins.

'So, you were taken …'

'Yes. He was tempted by his share of the gold they were going to take. It would have got us out, and all right again. But then he changed his mind,' Eloise went on.

'After they took it,' Squeaky concluded. It was not really a question. They wouldn't be after him if not.

'Yes. He got the gold, to look after it, but they didn't want to give him his share.' She looked Squeaky straight in the eyes as she said it.

For a moment, he believed her without question, then his common sense reasserted itself. 'That what he told you?'

'I saw it. And …' She hesitated. A bitterly painful memory, or a careful lie. 'I saw him fall in the river. Tide's swift there. And it's cold and dirty. Especially this time of the year. Bitter. Take your breath out of your body. He went down, and he never came up …' The tears were undeniably real this time. Unusually, she managed to weep without grimacing.

Squeaky could imagine how Worm would be

feeling. His heart would be aching for her. He had never had a father, or a mother, that he knew of, but sometimes dreams painted a softer picture than reality. He did not turn to look. He must concentrate on Eloise. Was she telling the truth? He stared hard at every line in her face. Her hands, still wet from the mop, rested on the table. He could not tell.

'They weren't there?' he asked. 'The old one and the young one?'

'No. They drove him there, lost him for a minute, but he knew they were after him and he had nowhere to go. They as good as killed him.'

'Where were you, that you saw this?'

'Next wharf over,' she said without hesitation. 'They came on to the other wharf just after he'd gone in.'

'They didn't see?'

'Yes, they did.'

'Two years ago? Then why are they only just getting nasty about it now? Don't make sense,' Squeaky pointed out.

'They were looking for me,' she said quietly, 'and they managed to find me. The only reason they haven't hurt me really badly is because I've told them my father is still alive.'

Worm was looking at her intently. 'Is he?'

She closed her eyes, but the tears still escaped. 'No. I told you. In effect they killed him when they chased him along one of the wharfs leading from the warehouse they own. But I told them they were wrong, that he went off the end all right, but on to the ledge below.'

He asked her what mattered, for this purpose now. 'And he had the gold with him?'

'No. He hid it somewhere. I don't know where it is, but I told them I did.'

'Why?'

Before she could answer, Worm interrupted, 'What's a ledge? What's it made of?'

She seemed confused.

Squeaky looked at her. 'I've never seen a ledge below a wharf. There's just water, and if you fell into the water … No one falls into the Thames around here, where there's mud and tides and eddies and stuff, and comes up out again alive.'

'They don't know that!' she said defiantly. 'Not as they can prove! He could be alive!'

'But he ain't, right? You've never seen him, that day to this,' Squeaky insisted.

There was a long moment's silence.

Worm looked from Eloise to Squeaky, a shadow across his face.

Squeaky hesitated. Should he let it go? No. He couldn't. If they followed this through, whatever it was, she would take her chance to avenge her father's death or, worse than that, she would create a chance. It had driven her this far already. She was living in a filthy wreck of a house. All her scrubbing would never make it clean. Decades of filth was probably what held it together. Either one of the two men could turn violent and ugly, awake whatever violence lay dormant in them from the beginning. When she didn't have the gold, and they found that out, what then?

Had she never thought that far?

Or did she know where it was?

No, that made no sense. She could have changed it for money a little at a time, and lived very nicely. She didn't even have to stay in London. She could go to any of a hundred smaller cities and disappear.

'You don't have the gold.'

She started to speak, then stopped abruptly. She did not know what to say. All answers put her in trouble. She needed to claim ignorance to put Squeaky off, and yet she needed to know where the gold was to inveigle the two men watching her into her plan. But to do what?

Was she after the gold? Or after revenge?

Squeaky looked at her face. It was strong, and yet curiously vulnerable. She was afraid. And she could not look at Worm. Did she have any idea of how beautiful she was to him? Not traditionally beautiful, in her eyes, her hair, her skin, the way she smiled – all things a man might notice. Worm thought he saw in her beauty of the mind, a purity and gentleness. Like any other child, he saw what he needed – what the Christmas story offered to him – the perfect mother figure.

Not a hurt woman greedy for gold, and above all for revenge.

Poor Eloise! Damn the two men who had hurt her so badly. Damn the sun for coming out in an instant, and when Worm was looking, to shine on her.

There was no time to think of something. Worm was waiting, watching her.

'We've got to catch them,' Squeaky said slowly. 'Or we've got to confuse them. Put them off. Separate them, perhaps.'

'Why?' Worm asked.

'Because they are after the gold, and Eloise doesn't have it, but they think that she knows where it is.'

'It's lost?'

'Yes. But they won't leave her alone until they believe that.' Would he see the hole in that argument?

Worm turned to Eloise. 'You don't have to stay with them. You don't have the gold, and your father can't be hurt any more. The river got him.'

She bit her lip. 'They think I have the gold because I told them that I did. If I say I don't now, they won't believe me.'

Worm looked at Squeaky. 'What are we going to do?'

Squeaky was backed into a corner. 'We confuse them. We make them doubt themselves. Your father … what was his name?'

'Horace,' Eloise replied slowly. She was staring at Squeaky. It made him slightly uncomfortable.

'What did he look like?'

She drew a deep, slightly shaky breath, and then let it out slowly. 'He looked a lot like you. Not as tall, but otherwise … well … if I turned round quickly, I could mistake you for him.'

Squeaky stared at her. She looked back completely innocently … didn't she? Was anyone so pure?

She read his thoughts and smiled. 'It's a good idea,' she said softly. 'I'm sure I can think of some things that will help. We had better start straight away. You will do it?' It was a question, but only just. She already knew he would.

There was no way out. Squeaky accepted, as if he had intended to all along. 'Let's start to plan ...'

The first thing was to create confusion. They began with thinking about the older man, Oldham, perhaps the more vulnerable. Eloise reiterated what Goldie had said: that he wanted to be important, known by everyone. Eloise assured Squeaky that it was not a wish to be liked. That did not come into it. To be feared was good, but to be known was what really mattered. You could build whatever you wanted to upon that.

To create an illusion that would take him in she also schooled Squeaky in little matters. 'Horace used to clear his throat a lot when he was angry or uncertain. When any kind of emotion was there. He had long hair, like yours, sort of ... untidy. Ran his hands through it, like you do sometimes. She smiled to rob the comment of any offence. 'I never saw him with a hat. You'll have to put that away.' She looked at his rather battered black hat with regret. 'Pity, it's nice. I'll find you a scarf for round your neck, one like his. He wore it a lot. Especially this time of year.'

Squeaky began to feel backed into a corner, but he accepted that it was necessary. If he was going to do this at all, then he should do it properly. It was more than a matter of price. He was growing increasingly aware that it might even become a matter of survival. These men, if they were caught for the death of Horace – and it might not have been an accident – coupled with the robbery of the gold, would be facing the rope. A short walk and a long drop, as people put it. He should not forget that. They wouldn't!

He could see very clearly now that it would have been immeasurably better if he had let Worm face the guilt for not helping Eloise, or the disillusionment that she was a liar and probably a lot of other things, too. Someone would let him down – someone already had – before he was grown up, never mind later on. He would survive it. He was not Squeaky's responsibility.

And yet he would probably do it again. He knew that, too.

'How did he walk?' he asked Eloise.

'What?'

'How did he walk? Can't you hear straight? Did he limp? Take long strides? Or short ones? Lean forward? Favour one foot over the other? Think, girl!'

118

She tried her best to hide a smile. Something about his wish to do it properly amused her. Perhaps at another time he would have seen the funny side of it. Not now.

'Well?' he demanded. 'The laugh's on us if we do it wrong!'

She cleaned the smile from her lips, but not her eyes. 'You're a proper artist, aren't you! You've done this before?'

'What I've done before is none of your business. What's the answer?'

'Turned his left foot in a bit, and I suppose he favoured the right, kind of guarded the left, if you know what I mean? And he leaned forward. Moved quick. I suppose that's how he got away from them.'

'And took the gold with him? So it's in the river?'

'No, I told you. It was hidden; they know that. Gold's heavy, mud's deep. If they knew it was in the river they wouldn't be after it still, and they must have known my father hadn't got the gold with him when he escaped from them at the wharf.'

Which still left the questions: did she want the gold ... or did she want revenge? Or did she somehow think she was going to get both? So much for the lady with the light in her hair!

Squeaky could not even look at Worm, who was watching all this, and listening. What did he believe now? Did he realise she was using him to get her revenge? Maybe he thought it was all right. He had never had a father. Maybe he thought all fathers were good, special, that they should be saved if possible, and if not, then at least vindicated? Or else avenged? How the hell was Squeaky going to explain all this to him?

And why was Squeaky not just walking away from it all, as any sane man would?

Because Worm believed she was innocent, and in danger. She *was* in danger.

But she was about as innocent as any other conniving little tart with money and revenge on her mind. And the ability to make daft little boys think she was some kind of an angel. No, that was not right. Angels could look after themselves. This woman was the sweet, gentle mother he didn't have, the one who would have loved him.

That was why Worm wouldn't let her down.

And why Squeaky, God help him, couldn't let Worm down.

'Pay attention, girl!' he snapped. He was furious with her, and with Worm, and most of all with himself. Of all of them, he was the one who should have known better. 'Like this?' He got up and walked a dozen paces or so, turning his left foot in, weight more on his right, and leaning a little forward, as if he were in a hurry. 'Well?' he said irritably.

'It's perfect,' she said with a little smile, and blinked several times. 'You look just like him.'

Squeaky intended to reply, but suddenly the right words escaped him. He did not want to impersonate a dead man whom this girl had loved, and who had been a thief, murdered for gold. He wanted to go home to Claudine's warm kitchen and have a cup of tea and a piece of cake.

'Well, come on, then!' he snapped. 'We haven't got all night! It'll be Christmas soon enough.'

*

Squeaky had spent all day before laying the ground-work for this adventure. It had to go exactly as he'd planned it, or it would not work. People had been prepared, and paid with a promise of a good Christmas dinner. There were going to be far more guests at Claudine's table than she had imagined. But Squeaky had ordered an extra goose or two, and ingredients

121

from which to make more plum pudding. The money would have to be put back sometime, but he always kept one or two little pieces aside, just in case of emergencies. This was certainly one.

He knew they would need more than a little assistance, so he had collected many debts, forgiven a few, on condition of help, and made a few more promises.

Now he took a deep breath, and set out.

Worm did the same, only he did not go alone. It was mid-afternoon, but already the light was beginning to fade as he set out with Eloise. Worm had a pretty good memory, a necessary thing if you were very uncertain about either reading or writing. Anyway, it was a bad time to find a piece of paper in your pocket and read what you were supposed to do.

Eloise could read, but she also preferred to trust her memory. And she knew her way around these streets, to lead someone, or mislead them.

They were to begin as soon as they could find Oldham and Younger, which was not difficult, since the two men had accepted the invitation of a drink with a street pedlar who owed Squeaky a favour. Before long they were there sitting on a bench just inside a pub called A Three-Legged Man.

Worm stood on the doorstep, hesitating. He must do this right. They were about to begin, and each of them depended upon the other two, and of course all the people Squeaky had bribed, or threatened.

'Go on,' Eloise said behind him. 'Just go in. Make sure they see you!'

He caught his breath, and almost choked himself, he swallowed so hard. He started through the door, letting in a blast of cold air, and making a much louder noise than he had intended to. He almost tripped over Oldham's feet. He had certainly made himself noticeable all right!

'Look where you're going, you stupid little ...' Oldham said angrily.

Worm stared at him, then remembered his part. He turned on his heel and ran head-first into Eloise as she came in through the door.

'You can't come in here!' he shouted, waving his hands at her. 'They'll see you!'

Eloise gave a cry of alarm, stared at Oldham as if she had seen a ghost, and then turn and blundered out, followed closely by Worm, who turned once just to make sure they were following. They were.

Eloise and Worm came out and stepped to the side. Oldham ran straight into a thin, elderly man with white hair flying in the cold wind, and one hand up to his face.

Oldham stopped instantly, gasping in astonishment, and Younger collided with him. 'Fool!' he said furiously. 'What's the matter with you?'

Oldham was peering at the old man with the white hair as if he couldn't believe his eyes, when the man pulled his coat collar around his ears and turned his back. When he turned round again, his face was completely different, and his hair was dark and slick. He carried a white kerchief in his hand, and slipped it into his pocket. He bowed and smiled.

'New to these parts?' he enquired pleasantly, although Oldham had nearly knocked him off his feet.

'No!' Oldham said, angry at himself for what he had thought he'd seen. 'I've lived here all my life!'

The man peered at him. 'Odd. I've never seen you.' And before he could be questioned any further, he sidestepped and was lost in the shadows.

Worm giggled, and then in case Oldham hadn't heard him, he did it again.

'What are you laughing at, you cheeky little sod?' Oldham lunged towards him to box his ears. This was exactly what Squeaky and Eloise had told him would likely happen.

Eloise put out her foot, very neatly, and Oldham fell forward, carried by the impetus of his own weight.

He went down on his hands and knees on the pavement. When he clambered up again, bruised and shaking with anger, Worm was out of sight, and Eloise was alone, staring at the two men, her eyes wide with amazement. She turned to Younger. 'What did you do that for?' she asked in disbelief.

Oldham shook himself. 'Where's the urchin?' he demanded.

'Which urchin?' She looked amazed.

'The one what came with you, you fool. He tripped me.' He stared around, but Worm had already disappeared round the corner, running as if for his life, leading Oldham and Younger on to the next unnerving scenario.

Worm was standing beside a street entertainer, a quick-change artist, who looked like an old woman with a tray of bootlaces to sell. Worm knew the tray folded up, and unfolded again as something else. He also knew that the street sign said something quite different from usual, at least two of the lamps had unaccountably not been lit, and it was getting darker by the minute.

Just down the road the usual corner had been

125

blocked by an overturned cart, and the pub sign there altered to read 'The King and Sixpence' instead of 'The Earl of Essex'.

Eloise was stepping backwards, slowly. She knew she had to stay always just out of reach. Then, when she knew Oldham and Younger were following her, she turned and walked a short distance up the street to where she knew Squeaky was waiting for her.

It was quiet. There was no horse-drawn traffic, no clop of hoofs. It was nearly dark now and in the distance the lights burned yellow and orange. There was going to be a frost tonight. The cobbles were already slippery here and there.

Suddenly the old woman with the tray of bootlaces was in front of the confused men. 'Please, sir, Mr Oldham, sir, something you could use? Surely you could use a—' She stopped suddenly. 'I'm so sorry, sir, I thought you were someone what I knew! Could have sworn … at a distance, you look just like him. Sorry to trouble you, sir.' She stepped backwards off the footpath on to the street, then stumbled up the step and all but ran away around the corner.

Oldham stood staring after her. 'Fool!' he muttered. 'Must be drunk!' He looked at Eloise. 'What are you staring at, then?'

She affected not to hear him, and followed after the woman, as if neither of the two men on the pavement were there at all.

Worm watched her, and as she came past him, grasped for her hand. 'You all right?' he whispered.

'He's as mad as a wet hen,' she said hurriedly. 'We'd better not get caught. We got to make sure he goes up the hill and past the other folks, so he doesn't know what to believe. We've only just begun. We've all the way to the warehouse yet, and it won't work if we don't get them there.'

'We'll do it,' Worm said, as if he were certain. He wanted to be.

They hurried up the street. It was a very slight incline, and Eloise kept hold of Worm's hand. It was not dark enough yet for them to lose each other, but it was nice to feel someone so close to you. There was no time to see if the men were following.

'Do you know where you are?' Worm asked as they came to a junction, and without hesitation she turned left again. They waited a few minutes, quite still and silent, until they saw the two men pass and go the other way, beginning to climb a little as the incline increased.

'Come on,' Eloise said suddenly. 'We've got to

follow them, just in case they don't go where I think they're going.'

Worm went obediently.

'Yes. I used to live here when I was a child,' she explained, slowing down a bit. 'Are they still ahead of us?'

He ran up the hill a few yards in the mist. He did not like it, but there was little chance Oldham would not be there, or Younger, closer than Worm would really have liked. He could not see anyone else. He dropped back to walk with Eloise, and gripped her hand a little more tightly.

Suddenly a donkey came out of a hidden entrance, a cart just behind it, piled high with all kinds of things. It was impossible to make out what they were in the misty dusk. An old man walked beside the animal, and they stopped on the footpath in front of the two men.

Eloise and Worm went into the arch of a doorway. The old man with the donkey had a coat that came all the way to the ground, not that that was far. He was very short, and he wore an immensely high top hat. 'Don't shout!' he said to no one in particular. He looked towards Oldham. 'Mr Tucker, is that you?'

'No, it isn't!' Oldham snapped. 'And get that bleeding thing out o' the way!'

'It's Christmas,' the old man said, as if that were a reasonable explanation for him standing in the middle of the path with a donkey. But he led it a little further out, so now it was blocking half the road, as well as the footpath.

'Get out of the way!' Oldham shouted at him.

'It's a long time till morning,' the old man said pleasantly. 'You've got no hurry.' He patted the donkey in a companionable fashion. 'Christmas'll come wherever you are, Mr Tucker, don't fret.'

'I'm not Tucker!' Oldham shouted even more loudly. He raised his hand, as if to strike the donkey.

The old man shot out his arm. 'You'd hit a donkey? On Christmas Eve? That's a terrible thing to do, Mr Tucker. It'll bring you bad luck for the rest of your life, I shouldn't wonder.' He turned to the donkey. 'Come along, Moke, this is a bad place. Bad things are going to happen here. I can feel it. The dead are coming back to collect what's theirs.' Suddenly the donkey seemed willing to move, quite quickly.

It put its weight against the load in the cart, and went forward at a brisk pace.

But the two men were not comforted in the least. In fact, they looked as if they had seen a vengeful ghost. They went forward, then stopped again. Worm and Eloise behind them were obliged to stop also, or risk being close enough to the men that they could not help but notice them.

Worm watched uncertainly, not at all sure what was going to happen next, or if their plan was such a good one after all. The two men were rattled, but what good was that going to do if they did not go on to the warehouse?

Then Oldham gasped and suddenly went rigid. Worm looked where he was staring. It was darker now, and the mist was rising, thicker in patches, a bit here, a bit there. It was horribly cold. An old man had come out of the one of the side alleys and was walking ahead of them. He had an odd gait, turning his left foot in, but not his right one. He was tall and thin, with straggly white hair and no hat, but he wore a thick scarf. He seemed to walk with a purpose, as if he were going somewhere in particular, and in a hurry. Once, very quickly, he glanced behind him and seemed to increase his pace. It was Squeaky, wasn't it?

Oldham stood on the pavement stock-still, as if momentarily paralysed.

Worm put his hand in Eloise's and felt her grip him hard. She looked as if she could hardly believe her eyes either.

The man ahead of them moved swiftly, for all his twisted left foot.

Suddenly, Oldham came to life and lurched forward, gathering speed as if he would catch up with the old man. He called out something unintelligible, but the man seemed to take no notice. There was a wraith of mist ahead of him and he walked into it as if he could see perfectly clearly. Younger followed them.

Worm and Eloise went forward, close behind the two men now. Worm had to run a couple of steps to keep up.

The old man with the limp disappeared into the mist, and Oldham went after him.

'Come on!' Eloise said urgently to Worm, half pulling him along. The mist closed round them like a damp clinging blanket. It prickled like needles of ice. Then suddenly they were through it and the night was clear again. Oldham was standing on the pavement, staring around himself. The other man, Younger, was disappearing ahead. The old man had completely vanished. There were no alleys off to the side, no deep doorways, and certainly none open. He had simply gone.

Worm and Eloise were too close. Oldham could not help seeing them.

131

Oldham took a step towards them, then realised they were a woman and a child. In the bad light of the waning day, the mist and the distortion of the streetlights reflecting on the wet pavement, throwing more reflections than shadows, he was uncertain and beginning to be frightened. He did not recognise them. His mind was focused on the spectre ahead of him, and some horror of the past.

Eloise kept walking, now pulling Worm along with her, as if they knew where they were going. They passed by Oldham as if they did not see him. Worm could feel the strength of Eloise's hand as she gripped him and he could not have let go even if he had wanted to. And he didn't!

Where was Squeaky? Still somewhere ahead of them?

They did not even turn to see if Oldham was right behind them, though that was difficult to resist.

'Don't worry,' Eloise whispered. 'I know it's Squeaky. At least I think I do. But he looks exactly like my dad.' Her voice was thick with emotion for a moment.

'Did your dad keep you safe?' Worm asked. Then he wished he hadn't. What if the answer was a bad one? What if he hadn't looked after her? People didn't always. Even dads. He had never had one, but he imagined. He could remember his mother a bit, but she kept changing the way she looked, as if she'd actually been several different people. But she talked a lot. Somewhere at the back of being comfortable, there was always a voice singing something. Often it didn't make sense, but it was a nice sound.

Eloise had not answered. Perhaps the answer was not a good one.

'Where'd he go?' Worm said instead. He meant Squeaky.

They walked up the street a little further. They had let Oldham pass them again in the poor light. He was ahead of them, and moving as if he knew exactly where he was going. He had not even looked at them. He turned a corner, went a hundred yards further, and turned again the other way. Eloise followed without hesitation. It was now completely dark, except for the streetlamps, some of which were broken. Worm looked, but he could not see the old man ahead of them. It *was* Squeaky, wasn't it?

'Are we lost?' he asked Eloise finally.

'No,' she answered with certainty. 'Oldham knows where he's going.'

'Where?'

'To the old warehouse on the river, where it happened.'

'How do you know that?'

'I just … know … This is what we planned.'

'Is the other man going to be there?'

'I don't know. Doesn't matter. Oldham will do.'

'Do for what?' He wasn't certain what she meant, but he had an awful idea. It wasn't all to do with the gold. There was something that mattered more than that, at least to Eloise, if not to Oldham.

Then it happened again. Oldham reached a fork in the road and seemed to be uncertain. Worm and Eloise were only a stone's throw behind him. The mist was thicker on the way to the left. He turned a little towards the right.

Eloise gasped. It must have been loud enough for him to hear, because he turned and stared straight towards them.

Eloise was looking down the street to the left, as if she had not even seen Oldham.

Worm looked the same way, and saw the old man with the flowing white hair again. He was staring back at them! Was it really Squeaky? It didn't look like him! Not really.

Worm froze. A cold wind blew off the street, damp

134

and with salt in its breath. They were getting closer to the river. From way to the south came the haunting sound of the foghorn, inhuman yet soaked through with a terrible loneliness.

The man with the limp put his hand up in the air. Was it a salute, or a threat? Then he laughed, and turned on his heel. He walked into a circle of lamp-light, and then out of it and into the mist. It was Squeaky. Worm recognised the laugh. He was visible for another instant, and then he vanished again.

Oldham, closer to them, let out a roar of rage that was swallowed in a racking cough, and then a sob.

'Papa!' Eloise called out and started forward, still clutching Worm by the hand. He had no choice but to go with her. Oldham overtook them in five strides. He was stronger, faster, and not encumbered by skirts, and dragging along a child. He barely noticed them. They could have been any homeless woman with her child. He raced down the footpath as if at last he knew the place he was going. He was not following a real man, or a ghost, he was going somewhere very familiar, that carried a horror, but also a prize that drove out everything from his mind.

Eloise was slowing up, and eventually she stopped, out of breath.

135

'It's only Squeaky,' Worm said to her, holding her hand now more than she was holding his.

'I know ...' she said quietly. 'Of course I do.'

'You said your dad was dead,' Worm reminded her, still holding on to her hand. Perhaps it was a cruel thing to say, but this was no time for pretending. Something in her frightened him. She was staring straight ahead of her, along the street where Oldham had run after the figure that had to be Squeaky.

'You did,' Worm insisted. 'You know Squeaky dressed up as your dad to scare Oldham. Why is he so scared of him, anyway?'

'Because Oldham killed him!' She forced the words out between her teeth, but with terrible satisfaction. 'He thinks it's Dad's ghost, come back to kill him for what he did!' Her face looked different in the light from the nearest streetlamp. There were tiny droplets of mist in her hair. 'He killed him,' she said slowly and very clearly. 'They chased him along the wharf and he fell into the river, and it closed over him ... dark, and filthy, and ice cold– like a grave itself. Only you go into it still alive ... and you know you'll never come out! It fills your eyes, and your ears, and your mouth ...'

'Stop it!' Worm tried to shout, but the words came out half strangled.

She said nothing. He looked at her face and saw the misery in it, and the hatred. Oldham had done that to her father, and to her it was as if it had been yesterday. Worm tried to think how he would feel, and he couldn't. It was too big, too terrible. All he could do was hold on to her hand, although he thought she couldn't even feel it.

'Come on,' she said, and started pulling him along again. 'We've got to keep up.'

'Why?' He pulled against her. 'You know Squeaky doesn't know where the gold is.'

'The gold?' She almost sounded as if she did not know what he meant.

'You want to get the gold back?' The moment the words were out of his mouth, he knew that was not what she really wanted. She wanted revenge. She was only using the gold, and the idea that Oldham would think Squeaky was the ghost of the man he had killed. Or perhaps the real man? Still alive somehow! Escaped from the mud of the river by falling on a ledge, as she had told him. And he would know where he had hidden the gold.

He pulled his hand away from hers. 'That's what you wanted Squeaky for. What happens if they kill him, too?'

'They won't! Worm! They won't!' She stopped. She was facing him now. 'They made that mistake the first time. They killed my father before knowing what he did with it! They won't kill him this time, until they know where the gold is.'

'Squeaky don't know where it is! How can he tell them anything?'

'He can't,' she said.

'Then what's he for?' As soon as the words were out of his mouth, he had a possible idea. 'You're not going to let them hurt him, are you?'

'No, of course I'm not!' But she did not look at him.

What was he going to do? He and Squeaky had come to rescue her! To stop Oldham and the younger man from keeping her prisoner. Or worse than that, hitting her. But she didn't know where the gold was, any more than they did. She was deliberately making them think that Squeaky was the ghost of her father – or maybe really her father, still alive and come back from wherever he had been to collect the gold. He was probably the only one who knew where it was, had always been, because he was with them when they took it. He was one of the thieves, in spite of the fact that she had said he wasn't.

If he were alive, though, and had been going to

give it back, he would have done that by now. He'd had a whole two years! Oldham would know that. It didn't make sense.

*

They were passing underneath a lamp-post and the yellow light, mist-swirled, gave them an eerie glow, making the shadows blacker. Her face was pinched, as if there was something inside her that filled her with pain. Seeing it, Worm was filled with it, too, and it frightened him. It changed her in a way he did not like.

'Come on,' she said. 'Or we'll lose them. I can look after myself.'

That felt like a dismissal, and yet she held on to his hand just as tightly, and they hurried after both men. Squeaky was somewhere ahead of them – Oldham, too – and perhaps the younger man as well.

They were close to the river now. The air was full of the smell of tidal water, mud flats and salt. The mist was blowing across them much more often. Sometimes it was completely clear, at other times there were heavy bands, like giant discarded shawls, floating across the street, obscuring cobbles and the roadway, wrapping the streetlamps until they were almost hidden. Then in a breath of wind, they were just white shades pulling to bits in the distance. There were several people visible now and then, including Oldham's angry figure. All were black, and then ahead of them Squeaky, white hair flying, arms and legs at angles, limping on his left foot.

Worm knew where they were going.

The buildings around them were huge now, with wide doorways a horse and cart could pass through. And they towered upwards three or four storeys, some of them more, with no windows. These were warehouses, for storing things that came and went in the big ships in the docks, and waiting in the Pool of London. Were they empty? Or full of things from foreign places?

Nobody lived around here. There were no coloured lights or busy people preparing for Christmas tomorrow, no carol singers, and it was far too early for the church bells.

Worm hurried along with Eloise. She was not just following Oldham; she knew where she was going, too.

The mournful boom of a foghorn sounded again. The fog must be worse on the water. They were very close to it now, and Worm could feel the icy tingle of droplets on his face.

Squeaky had disappeared somewhere ahead. The only person Worm could see in front was Oldham.

'Come on,' Eloise said again urgently. 'We're nearly there!'

'Where?' he asked. But he had a horrible feeling that he already knew. 'This was where your dad died, isn't it?'

'Yes,' was all she said.

Worm could feel through the grip of her hand that her arm was rigid now. Probably, her whole body was.

The warehouse they were nearing towered over them in the gloom. Even looking upwards, Worm could not see the top of it against the darkness of the sky. It was as if they were shut inside a box already, and the lid was on.

Eloise pulled him in through the side entrance, and immediately he felt the difference. There was no more wind, or tiny little pinpoints of ice. The air was perfectly still, but it smelled strange, stale, as if it had been breathed in and out by somebody else before, someone very tired, and dirty all through.

'Where are we going?' Worm whispered.

'After them,' Eloise answered. 'Come on.' She took his hand again, probably so he wouldn't get lost and she would have to come back and look for him. Or more likely, so that they wouldn't find him and use him against her. Would she stop herself from hurting them, if they had Worm? He didn't want to ask that, because he honestly wasn't sure that she would. She hated them more than she liked Worm, that was for certain.

He kept up with her, even though she was going somewhere he didn't really want to go.

She stopped suddenly. They could hear men's voices ahead. It was Oldham and Younger. Younger must have been waiting here already. Worm could not see them, but he could hear them quite clearly.

'Where'd the old bastard go to?' Younger asked. He was obviously confused.

'To where Horace kept his things, of course!' Oldham replied. 'He'd hide the gold somewhere round here. Stands to reason.'

'Oh, very clever,' Younger said sarcastically. 'Like we didn't look there before! Turned the place inside out and found nothing.'

'If the old swine is still alive, where better to hide it than where we've already looked? Stupid!'

'Then what took you two bleeding years to work that out?' Younger said with an edge of ridicule to his voice.

''Cos I thought he was dead,' Oldham snarled.

'Who told you he wasn't dead, then?'

'Eloise, of course! What do you think we took her for?'

'Well, I know what I think you took her for!'

'You ever tried that with her? And don't bother lying to me. I know where you got that bite on your arm. And it weren't rats!'

'I'll do her next time.'

'And then what? If so, you'll have to kill her, or she'll come after you!'

'So I'll kill her, then! What's wrong with that? We don't need her, after we've got the gold. Only took her so we could find the old man. What do you reckon brought him back?'

''Cos he left the gold here, you fool! He didn't come back for her, that's for sure. He would've taken her with him the first time. Silly little cow!'

Worm felt Eloise wince beside him. It wasn't so much a movement as a tightening of everything inside her, as when one expects a blow. That was nothing like the father she had described. Did she not remember, and put it in her mind as she wished it had been? He could understand that. He felt a fierce twinge of pity for her. It hurt. It hurt very much.

143

Then he thought of what the men meant to do to her. He'd seen men hurt women before, just because they liked to. Some of those screams he would not forget.

He pulled hard at her hand. 'Do we have to get the gold? If we leave them, they'll find it anyway, and then kill each other over it,' he urged.

'I need to see it,' she said harshly. 'I want to make sure they find it. Or if they don't, then they'll each think the other got to it first.'

'What about Squeaky?'

'Don't worry. He'll get away.'

Even as she said it, Worm knew she was lying. She was so angry, she'd forgotten about Squeaky. He was going to have to do something about this himself. He tried to slip his hand out of hers, but she held on too tightly.

They both stiffened as they heard the movement ahead. Then suddenly there was a scraping sound and a tiny pinprick of light appeared. One of them had struck a match, and a scene gradually took form around them. At first it was only a hand holding a taper in front of a lantern, the glass shiny and smeared. The taper touched the wick and a yellow glow filled the lantern and beyond. They could see

Oldham's face, all planes and angles, dark smudges where his eyes must be, black brows, stubble on his cheeks and chin.

Younger was crouched near him. He was smiling, the light shining on his teeth and reflecting in his eyes, as if they were blue glass.

Eloise gripped Worm's hand even harder.

Where was Squeaky? Was he here? Was he watching and listening too? Was he safe?

Worm had no idea how high the ceiling was, or the roof. He could see only a short distance around the two men, maybe four feet in each direction. Two men crouching over a lantern, a couple of wooden boxes, both broken, and the contents scattered. Beyond the light other boxes and bales rose like shadows, no more than an impression of height, of darkness arching above endlessly – in a ceiling? A roof? Not the sky, because it was dry in here, without wind or air, but still bitterly cold.

For long seconds, nobody moved.

Where was Squeaky?

Worm gripped Eloise's hand.

Then from somewhere in the darkness close above them, the sound of laughter. Then it came again, softer the second time, but quite clear.

Oldham shot to his feet, the lantern swaying violently. The light moved all round the cavernous interior of the warehouse. There were boxes and bales in the centre of the floor, but a lot of the outer walls were bare. Perhaps they were waiting for a shipment? There was a first floor, fifteen feet higher at least, and a flight of wooden stairs running up to its balcony. The faint glimmer of a lantern shone on Squeaky's white hair. He looked like an animated skeleton, with his bony hands, fingers outstretched, and his cadaverous face smiling now, all his long uneven teeth showing. His arms and legs were invisible.

Younger let out a shriek, but whether it was anger or terror, or both, Worm couldn't tell, and he didn't care. Squeaky was all right, and he was here with them.

Squeaky waved, then backed away from the railing and disappeared out of sight, and they heard the clatter of his feet as he ran along the balcony and down a passageway.

Both the other men scrambled up the stairs after him, the lantern waving and jerking wildly, at risk of shattering any moment, as the darkness closed in.

Eloise jerked Worm so hard he tripped and regained his footing only with difficulty and had to catch up with her. She was following the men with the lantern, and it was easy enough to see where they were. It was entirely another matter for Worm to see his own way up the stairs. They reached the top and went along the same passageway. Eloise fell over a bale of something and landed hard, pulling Worm with her. But she was so bent on keeping up with Oldham and Younger that she didn't even make a cry. She climbed to her feet again, grasped for Worm, and ran even faster to catch up.

The wavering light was ahead of them, getting higher in the air as Oldham climbed another flight of steps, cursing softly as he went.

Worm's legs were aching, but the alternative to keeping up was being left alone in the vast cavern, with no idea where the others were – miles away, gone home without him, or creeping up on him in the dark. And anyway, he had to be with Eloise, because she was going towards something dreadful and she needed Worm to save her from it. No one else would, not even Squeaky, because he didn't know what she meant to do.

They banged into the bottom of more stairs, bruising themselves. But there was no time to think of pain. Immediately they started to climb up even

147

higher. The light disappeared ahead of them. That must mean everyone had gone further in: Squeaky with the first light, Oldham with the second.

The steps were steep; Eloise had to hold up her skirts so she didn't trip over them. It would be terrible to fall all the way down to the bottom. You could break your neck and be dead. Worm concentrated on climbing.

They reached the top and stopped to catch their breaths, both of them. It was a long way up. Counting the first, it was now three normal flights at least. He looked around. It was just as cold up here, but greyer, not black, as if there were lights somewhere ahead, grey light at the upper storey. And he could smell the mud and salt more sharply now. He leaned towards the cold air and saw dimly the black outline of the warehouse walls against an opening to the sky.

He felt Eloise's fingers tighten on his arm. There was a tiny yellow light ahead of them. Squeaky – or Oldham?

'Go carefully,' Eloise whispered.

'They can't see us,' Worm answered. 'We got no light, and it's dark anyway.'

'It's very dark,' she agreed. 'And if we fall over anything, sure as death, they'll hear us.' She pulled him a little as she stepped forward with the same confidence as if she could see. Did she know where she was going? Did she know everything, even where the gold was, and she was just pretending?

They moved softly, all the way along the passage, smelling the open air more strongly with each yard they covered.

Suddenly Eloise stopped and jerked Worm to a standstill beside her.

He froze. And then he heard a voice. It was Oldham and he sounded frightened and angry.

'Don't stand there gibbering and pointing your hands! You're not a ghost, damn you!'

There was no answer. Was he speaking to Squeaky? He must be.

'Where is it?' Younger said loudly. 'You left it here!'

'He didn't,' Oldham argued, and his voice filled with contempt. 'He came back after we'd searched, and left it here then!'

'Why would he do that?'

'How in hell do I know? Perhaps because we were after him and he knew we'd already searched here?'

'Lot of good that did us!'

'Well, maybe the bleeding police were after him!'

149

Then came the quite distinct sound of laughter.

Squeaky again?

'Be careful,' Worm whispered. 'Oh, be careful you ...' He could not think of the right words. He wanted to say 'fool' but that was disrespectful and he did not feel that way about Squeaky. Squeaky was only here because Worm had followed a silly dream, and Squeaky had followed him with it, to keep him safe. He could see that now.

'We've got to help,' he whispered to Eloise.

'Shh!' she hissed, but she pulled him with her several more steps in silence.

Worm stumbled a few times, but they moved all the way along the passage without any chance to see the ground. But at the far end, the light was grey, as if beyond them the sky had light in it. Maybe the clouds had blown away, at least in part, so the moon could be out.

Eloise stopped. She touched Worm in warning and he said nothing. They were on a sort of balcony and looking down a few wooden steps to a small work-room. There were two lanterns lit, both resting on the floor. It gave the space an eerie look, everything lit from beneath instead of above, as they were used to. Faces looked different, yellow light under the chin, making the eyes look like holes in the head, noses and cheekbones exaggerated. All the planes of their faces were gold, heads shapeless at the back in the darkness. Hands cast huge shadows.

Oldham and Younger were both scrabbling in old drawers and boxes. Squeaky was well apart from them, watching. He looked exaggeratedly tall in the misplaced light, as if his head were seven or eight feet above those of the men on the floor, moving so feverishly.

No one looked up long enough to see Eloise or Worm. Worm looked sideways at her. They should have seen her, because the lantern light, even at a distance, caught her face at the periphery of its range, and caught the gold in her hair.

Worm pulled her back a bit, and she seemed to understand why.

Younger finished going through one old chest of drawers, many of the drawers broken, and there was no use trying to put them back in the frame. He swore, and moved to a crate. He seemed unaware of Squeaky watching him, never mind Eloise and Worm. He began to pull the crate apart.

Oldham looked around, checking that Younger was still looking, then resumed his own search.

151

Seconds ticked by.

Then suddenly Oldham gave a shout.

Everyone turned to stare at him. He was pulling straw out of a packing case, and when he was at the bottom, he very carefully lifted out a metal box. It was as if he knew the gold was inside it, he lifted it so gently, and with such a look of glee in his yellow, lantern-lit face.

Younger threw aside the crate he had been working on, hurling it a distance away and disregarding its splintering against the side of another wooden crate. He dived forward.

Far above them, Squeaky was watching intently.

Eloise stood so still, Worm wondered if she were breathing. Her hand gripped his so hard it hurt. He wriggled a bit, but she was oblivious of him. All she could see was her father's metal box.

Oldham pulled the lid, but it did not move. He pulled again.

Younger swore sharply and snatched the whole box from him. He exerted his entire strength, but the box lid did not budge. He picked up the box, and from his sudden bending Worm knew it was really heavy. Was it full of gold? Really full?

For a long moment Oldham and Younger stared at each other.

Worm felt Eloise let go of his hand and move away a step. On the other side of the room, at the same height as themselves, Squeaky took a step forward, lifted up his hand for a moment, and smiled. Then he stepped out of the light, and when Worm looked again, he had disappeared.

On the floor where Oldham and Younger were still trying to open the box, Oldham shook it and something heavy and metallic rattled inside. Oldham's face gleamed with the thought of triumph.

That was when Worm turned and looked at Eloise. She had moved a step further forward and her face was clearly visible in the light of the two lanterns below. She looked as if she had finally tasted a long-hungered-for victory. A wide smile curved her lips. It was not sweet or gentle; it was a smile shining with satisfaction. In fact it was unkind.

'So, you found it?' she said.

Oldham drew his breath in sharply, and coughed hard. It was dusty in here.

'Yeah,' he said, smiling back at her as if he had known she was somewhere close. 'Didn't think we would, did you?'

He lifted the box and rattled it. 'Hear that? It's gold!'

Eloise began carefully going down the steps, one and then stopping, another and then stopping. 'Yes,' she agreed. 'Yours – and his.' She gestured towards Younger. 'Say half and half. Or maybe you want a bit more than that? You did most of the clever stuff, after all.'

'Hey!' Younger rose to his feet, his face twisted with fury. 'I done the dangerous bits. Who are you fooling?'

Oldham stood up too, his skin flushed dark with anger. 'So you're wanting more than half? You'll get your share, and no more!'

'Gonna make me, are you?' Younger shouted back, lifting his fist.

Worm looked sideways at Eloise. He expected to see fear in her face – he wanted to – but what he saw was satisfaction. They had killed her father, and now they were going to kill each other. For the gold? Or just for hate?

He took her sleeve and pulled at it hard. 'You can't let them do this! Eloise!'

'I can. They killed my father for that. Then they can kill each other now.' There was no softness in her. Only anger and terrible pain.

It brought a hard lump to Worm's throat, and an

154

ache he couldn't send away. But he was caught, too big to cry like a little boy. He swallowed. 'Then you're no better than them!'

She swung round to look at him.

He was furious because he couldn't stop the tears spilling over and running down his cheeks.

'I suppose you want me to stop them?' she said.

He couldn't speak, his throat was too choked, but he nodded.

Just below them, Oldham and Younger were shouting at each other. Oldham took a swing and the punch landed hard. Younger staggered backwards.

'Stop it!' Eloise shouted. Letting go of Worm, she went quickly down the last few steps and over towards them.

Oldham hit her and she almost fell over.

'Idiot!' she said back at him, forcing the words through her teeth. 'You can't even get into the box!'

They both stared back at her.

'Get out, Eloise. We don't need you any more,' Younger said bitterly. 'However much is for him or me, there's none for you. Go, while you can.'

'You won't get into it without me,' she said steadily.

'Oh, yeah?' he sneered. 'And then you'll just go away?'

She hesitated only a moment. 'Or you stand here and wonder how to get into a locked box, without asking someone you've got to pay ... or worse ... share it with. Thought of that?' She raised her eyebrows with both curiosity and sarcasm in her expression.

'What do you want for it?' Oldham asked. He took a step towards her.

'To walk away,' she answered. 'With the boy.'

'That'll cost you double.'

'Double what?' she asked. 'Two nothings is nothing! I'll get the box open for you.' She coughed as the dust caught in her throat.

'Open it,' Oldham roared at her.

She turned round to Worm, who was about a yard behind her. 'You go now,' she told him very seriously. 'You have to promise me, and keep your word, or they won't let me go. Do you understand? Do you know what a promise is?'

'Yes,' he nodded.

'You can keep a promise?'

'Yes ...'

'Open the damn thing!' Younger shouted at her. 'What's all this bleedin' dust in here?'

'It's just flour,' Oldham snapped back at him. 'Shut up, and bring the box.'

'Worm!' Eloise said sharply. 'Promise! You've got to go ... now!'

'What about you?' he asked.

'I've got to worry about them, not you. Go!'

Slowly he turned and walked away, but the moment he was in the shadows he stopped and looked back. Then after a moment, he crept round the side, towards where Squeaky had been, and looked over.

Eloise was standing near the box, and she had something in her hand with a sharp point. She kneeled down and put the point of it into a hole at the back of the box. She moved it around for several moments, then at last the lid opened.

Oldham snatched the box from her and put his hand inside it. He pulled out a piece of metal. It was grey, dull.

'It's lead!' he shouted in disgust. He threw it away and thrust his hand back in. He pulled out another grey piece. 'What's this?' he yelled at Eloise.

She took a step back, and then another. 'It's pewter,' she replied. 'He was a pewter smith, remember?'

Younger snatched the box from Oldham and turned it upside down.

Worm could see that the box must be heavy. No wonder they had believed there was gold in it!

157

Eloise was slowly moving away from them.

Oldham hit the box and swore. Younger snatched it from him again and hit it hard.

Eloise crept silently up the stairs, and when she reached the top she went swiftly into the darkness of the passage.

Younger hurled the box as violently as he could, cursing at the top of his voice. It hit the railing and struck hard at the metal bands of a keg.

Worm saw the glint of gold, soft, yellow gold where the pewter coat had been broken, just before the blinding flash blew him off his feet and hurled him to the ground.

Where was Eloise? He scrambled up again, bruised, but nothing worse. It might hurt later, but now it was no worse than when he fell off a bale in the dock.

He had no idea where Squeaky was, but he must find Eloise, because she might be hurt. He kept his hand on the wall and followed it back a few yards, to where the passage was, turned down it, and went as fast as he could along the way he had seen her go.

He saw her ahead of him, and suddenly it was so bright he could see her quite clearly, because everything was bright, as if they were in the middle

158

of a lantern, and the noise was terrible, just about deafening.

He ran into Eloise and clung on to her as they were both thrown on to the floor.

She struggled to get up, gripping on to him. 'Where the hell have you been?' she demanded furiously.

'I went round to see if you were all right,' he answered, trying to stand up.

'Round what?'

'Round to where Squeaky was. What happened?'

She pulled her skirt straight and took his hand again. 'We've got to get out of here. They're after us. They're mad because there's no gold here. What's this now?' She raced back along the passage.

Worm turned to look and saw the scarlet flames. That's what the noise was, and the light. The whole room they had been in was on fire.

The sound of it was getting louder, and hotter.

'Come with me!' she said urgently. 'Run!'

'We've got to find Squeaky!' he protested.

There was another explosion, and part of the wooden balcony crumpled up and fell to the floor below.

This time he didn't argue. Hand in hand, they ran as fast as they could.

There was a yell of rage behind them, but there was no way to know if it was of fury at the fire, at Eloise and Worm, or each other.

There was also a crackle of flames tearing at the structure of the rooms, at wooden crates and barrels, at anything fire could consume.

Worm clung on to Eloise and they fled, stumbling now and then, even falling, but bruises were barely felt. They must find the way out. It was not dark any more, but orange red from the flames, and choking with smoke.

'Hurry,' she urged, pulling him even harder. 'We've got to get out while we can.'

He pulled back. 'But what about Squeaky? We can't leave without Squeaky!'

'Are they after us?' she gasped.

'They got the gold!' he insisted.

'No, they didn't. Didn't you see? The box was empty.'

'Yeah, I know, but it were made of gold.'

'What!' She was so startled she actually stopped running.

'We've got to find Squeaky! We can't go without him!'

'He probably got out another way. If Oldham

catches us he'll kill us. No use arguing about gold now. There is none.'

They could both hear Oldham shouting not far behind them.

'The box were made of gold,' Worm replied. 'When he threw it away, it landed on something hard, and left a scratch on it – deep. And it showed gold. He were a clever one, your dad.'

Oldham's voice was getting really close. 'Find that bitch and finish her this time. If we're going to burn, so is she!'

That shocked Eloise into starting to run again, pulling Worm along faster than his feet could find a grip on the uneven floor.

They turned a corner just as another part of the building gave way and crashed three storeys of burning wood down into the alley.

'No, not that way!' Eloise jerked Worm so hard that this time he did fall. It hurt.

She stooped and pulled him to his feet. 'I don't know the way. But we've got to hurry! There's sacks and sacks of flour in there. They could all explode. We've got to get away. Squeaky wouldn't want you to get killed. He might even be waiting for us outside.' She tore a bit off her skirt, yanking at it so hard it hurt her hands. She left it on the doorway, like a sign, then turned and grabbed hold of Worm's hand again. 'We've got to hurry. The fire is coming this way, and when it reaches here it will almost certainly blow up.'

He followed her because he really had no choice. It was hot and smoky, and the noise of burning was closer and louder. Oldham and Younger were also getting closer, and Worm was really frightened of them. He knew Oldham would hurt them both dreadfully if he could catch them. And they could run faster, and were much stronger. Worm couldn't save Eloise, and he couldn't save himself. And he couldn't bear to think of Squeaky in all the flames.

His lungs were bursting; his throat ached with the smoke in the air and the hot, acrid taste.

They must be nearly returned to the way out by now, surely!

He pulled back. What if Squeaky were in there, where the flames were?

Then he would be dead. That thought was too much to bear.

If he were there, then Eloise would go back for him – wouldn't she? Even though he was slowing her up, she wouldn't let him die?

162

Then before he could think of anything more, there was an explosion like the sound of a bomb. A terrible roaring noise. Worm was picked right up off the ground and hurled into the air as if he were never going down again. And then the cold ground hit him harder than he had ever fallen before. No one had ever hit him like that.

It was long, breathless seconds before he could even move. Then he sat up slowly and saw the biggest fire of his life. The whole back of the warehouse was gone and flames were roaring up into the sky, brilliant, white-hot in the heart, yellow, orange and red all around the place, and smoke, towers of smoke like the biggest fireplace in the world.

Where was Eloise? He tried to stand up, but he was too dizzy.

Then out of nowhere there was water all over the place, on the ground, big fountains of it in the air, all going towards the flames.

Somebody grabbed him and he tried to shout, but his throat was too dry. He was carried, wriggling as much as he could, and against his will, by a big man in a coat that felt funny. Then he was put down on the cobbles, but where he could see the horses of the fire engine standing nervously, breathing hard,

163

shifting their weight from one hoof to the other, big fire wagons just behind them. There was another wagon twenty yards away. At each of them there were men talking softly to the horses, telling them they would be all right.

It was a fireman who had carried Worm off the pavement where the explosion had thrown him.

'Eloise!' He forced his voice to come. 'Where is she?'

The fireman gave him a cup of water. 'You hurt?' he asked.

'No. Where's Eloise?'

'Over there,' the fireman pointed. 'She's a bit singed around the edges, but she'll be all right. Anyone else in there?'

'Yes. An old man with a jacket and no hat. White hair. Something lit up with a terrible bang – again and again. Please, you go to find him ...'

'We'll look. Anyone else?'

'Yes. Two bad men. It was them that made it burn ... You got to look for Squeaky ...'

The fireman's face was suddenly soft with pity. 'There's no one left alive in there now. Flour ... it can explode something terrible if it fills the air, if it's stale enough for that – but it's really bad.' He

164

stood up. 'You stay here. Do as you're told! Not getting you out of there a second time.'

Worm was very glad to do as the man told him. He was burned in all sorts of places. His chest hurt when he breathed, and so did his throat. He wondered about Squeaky. It mattered. It mattered desperately about Squeaky — it was none of it any use if Squeaky didn't come out alive. It hurt more than anything else.

Eloise hadn't taken her revenge. That was good. In fact, it was better than good. And the gold wouldn't belong to anybody. That was good, too.

When Eloise made her way over to him in the red light that filled the air, she found him crying silently.

'You seen Squeaky?' he asked with a sudden lurch of hope.

She shook her head. 'There's nobody alive in there now. I'm … I'm sorry …'

'So are we going home now?' he asked her, getting up with great difficulty, staggering a bit, when she caught him.

'Yes,' she answered with certainty, although she had no idea where home would be. She stepped forward and put her arms around him and hugged him, then, 'Where's home?' she asked.

'Come with me. It's in Portpool Lane. It's …' Then

he thought about Squeaky again and his eyes filled with tears. 'It's where Squeaky and I live ...' He daren't go any further.

She stroked his hair gently, but she could not find any words of comfort. Perhaps in her own way she felt just as bad?

He sniffed and pulled away from her. 'He could be in there. We shouldn't just go ...He ... he was getting ready for Christmas. He liked it. This one was going to be special.'

'It's just about Christmas Day now,' she answered. 'I reckon it's the middle of the night, and that's when it starts. He wouldn't want you to spend his special Christmas sitting in a pool of water, watching the warehouse burn down, would he?'

Worm shook his head, but his throat was too tight to speak.

'Let's go,' she said gently.

'It's a long way from here.' He refused to move. The argument didn't matter, and they both knew it. There could be no real Christmas without Squeaky.

Eloise waited several moments. 'It's too hot to stay here,' she said, as another gout of flame roared up into the sky.

He stood up and took her hand, and together they

walked away slowly. They were at the end of the street, still lit by the red glare, almost like daylight, when they were caught up by the scruffiest figure even Worm had ever seen before. His trousers were torn in several places, and scorched, his once-elegant coat singed up one side and minus one of its sleeves. His hair was burned and full of black bits on one side. His cadaverous face was smeared with soot, and one or two red patches where flying cinders had burned him. But he was smiling.

'Squeaky!' Worm cried out, and flew into his arms, hugging him with all his strength, clinging on to him as if he would never let him go.

Squeaky started to complain, then changed his mind and lifted Worm up and held him. Over Worm's shoulders he glanced at Eloise and dared her to say anything at all.

She didn't. She just started walking very slowly towards the better-lighted part of the street.

Squeaky put Worm down and together they caught up with Eloise.

'You coming for Christmas, then?' Squeaky said matter-of-factly. 'We're having roast goose. And pudding. And cake. And there are red ribbons all over the place.'

'Please?' Worm added.

'I'd like that,' Eloise replied hesitantly, looking from one to the other of them, trying to read in their faces if they really meant it.

And as they walked under the streetlamp, the glow caught the tears in her eyes and the light in her hair, a little singed, but still shining. And somewhere in a church tower, not far away, the bells began to ring.

*

Whatever Squeaky and Claudine had told Worm about Christmas, the reality far surpassed his imaginings. Everyone was smiling as, beside the decorated tree, the holly with its berries, the Nativity scene, and the enormous red satin bows that Worm had helped tie so proudly, they sat down to the festive feast. He thought all the geese in London must be crisply steaming on this table in Portpool Lane.

'Couldn't risk running short, could we?' Squeaky said, carving a generous portion. 'Pass that down to Eloise ...'

Spooning roast potatoes on to his plate – and nobody counting how many – Worm thought this was the best day of his whole life.

'Shall we raise a toast?' Squeaky asked Claudine.

'We shall indeed,' she agreed, glancing around the table at the people who had come to mean so much to her. She stood and everyone else did, too, including Worm, who wasn't sure what was going to happen next. 'Raise your glasses, everyone. A very Merry Christmas to you all!'

'A very Merry Christmas,' they echoed.

When the geese, the stuffings and vegetables, the sauces and the gravy, and the puddings – better, even, than spotted dick – had been eaten, and everyone was sitting around feeling drowsy and full, Worm decided it was the moment to give Claudine her present.

'I got you this,' he said shyly. 'It's to say thank you … for everything wot you've done for me.'

Claudine looked surprised but pleased. She took the little parcel, carefully untied the red ribbon and pulled away the gold paper. Her eyes were huge and suspiciously bright as she took out the scarf with the roses and carefully held it up.

'Oh, Worm … oh, it's beautiful,' she breathed. 'Thank you.' She leaned over to hug him and kiss his cheek. Then she draped the scarf loosely around her shoulders so that she could admire the pattern and feel its softness. 'Thank you … I've never seen anything so pretty.'

'I'm so glad you like it,' he said.

'I love it, Worm,' she replied.

He sank down beside her chair and rested his head on her knee, thinking through the wonderful day he'd had, starting with the church bells at midnight. This moment, though – this very minute – was what he would choose to remember for ever.